'For how long would this arrangement last?'

'Long enough to convince the lawyers that our marriage was genuine.' Luc shrugged. 'A year might be sufficient. Play the game according to the rules and your reward will be great.'

'I could always refuse to play at all.' Aphra returned his gaze.

'No, not you. I think I know you better than that. If the stakes are high enough, you'll play. And in this case we both know how high they are... So, Aphra, do we shake on it?'

Angela Wells was educated in an Essex convent, and later left the bustling world of media marketing and advertising to marry and start a family in a suburb of London. Writing started out as a hobby, and she uses backgrounds she knows well from her many travels, especially in the Mediterranean area. Her ambition, she says, in addition to writing many more romances, is to spend more time in Australia—especially Sydney and the islands of the Great Barrier Reef.

A CONVENIENT BRIDE

BY
ANGELA WELLS

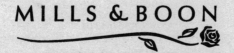

MILLS & BOON

First published in Great Britain 1996
Harlequin Mills & Boon Limited,
Eton House, 18-24 Paradise Road, Richmond, Surrey TW9 1SR

© Angela Wells 1996

ISBN 0 263 79961 1

Set in Times Roman 11 on 12 pt.
02-9702-51640 C1

Printed and bound in Great Britain
by Mackays of Chatham PLC, Chatham

CHAPTER ONE

APHRA stretched her slender body and, closing her eyes, turned her face skywards to enable the sun, newly emerging from a bank of dark clouds, to lay its first warming rays on her upturned face.

Drawing in a deep, appreciative gulp of the cool, fresh air, she enjoyed the heady fragrance of the mock-orange blossom, always at its most stunning after a heavy shower, as was the perfume of the Bourbon roses, although the rain would already have ruined their delicate natural beauty, turning the fat buds brown before they'd had a chance to open.

Sighing a little at the cruelty of nature, she strolled across the walled garden, lifting heavy boughs as she passed, to relieve them of the strain of so much rainwater, stopping now and again to kneel on the damp grass to reach for some weed that had rooted since last the gardener had hoed the rich dark soil.

How deeply Amélie Benchard had loved Fairmead Hall, she recalled nostalgically; how especially had she delighted in the enclosed rose-garden, adding to its formal beauty a selection of scented shrubs, which would, no doubt, have appalled the purists but which had given her untold pleasure in her latter years.

'I was born and spent my childhood in Corsica,' had been her simple explanation. 'There the perfume of the maquis is a constant companion of life. Here, in England, I cannot expect your pale sun to give to me what I miss so much, so I must find another means of providing myself with nature's perfume, *non, ma chère*?'

Aphra's full, warm mouth, bare of cosmetics, turned in a reminiscent smile as she remembered Amélie's small, determined face, the skin brown and wrinkled beneath the silver-flecked darkness of her hair.

'It is always true in life, is it not?' She'd pursued Aphra's approval. 'If one cannot have exactly what one wants, then one settles for second best and does not rest until it becomes first best!'

Certainly her employer and friend had carried out her maxim as far as the rose-garden was concerned, Aphra accorded, her eyes intent on the upper branches of one of the trees where she thought she'd detected the sweet note of a song-thrush.

Over the past nine months she herself had become as enchanted with this particular spot of the Hall's large grounds as the young woman who had first entered them as a bride of eighteen over sixty years ago, lonely and apprehensive, without a word of English to her tongue.

Aphra sighed. Now her own days here were limited. Soon the Hall, with its elegant Georgian architecture, would have a new owner and she would be cast out of her quiet paradise, back into the realities of life without Peter and without a job.

Finding employment shouldn't have been difficult for a person with her qualifications, but local authorities were drastically cutting their budgets, so it might be a struggle to find the kind of work for which she'd been trained.

Still, with perseverance she would succeed, but Peter... She blinked away a self-indulgent tear, raising her fist to blot the dampness from her cheek, oblivious to the muddy trail she left in its place. Peter's death had left a void in her life which even Amélie's brand of affection and hard common sense had only just begun to bridge.

A low, grumbling growl close at hand brought her attention back to the present.

'What's up, Sherlock?' The Alsatian had taken up a guard position, slightly in front of her, its hair bristling, its ears pricked as it stared at the open archway in the red-brick wall.

Another low growl came from his throat as she placed a restraining hand on his collar, then the sinking sun was blotted out as the arch was filled with the presence of a man.

Luc Benchard! Even silhouetted against the fading light, he was unmistakable—the broad shoulders, which in his youth had wielded a cricket bat to such devastating effect, clothed in a soft black leather jacket; the long, muscled legs, which had run such successful sponsored half-marathons for charity, clad in equally sombre trousers.

She couldn't make out his features but his hair was the same—black, soft and wavy, a legacy of his Corsican heritage—and his casual, impertinent grace was indisputable as he lounged between the pillars, one hand in a trouser pocket, the other balanced lightly on the brickwork.

She'd always known she would recognise him again if they met. What she hadn't anticipated was the painful way her heart kicked in her chest, the way her hands began to tremble and her pulse to race as if she were still the love-struck child who'd adored him from the moment when, as a summer visitor to the village at the age of eight, she'd watched him win the village cricket match almost single-handed.

He would have been seventeen at the time, she mused, and still at public school, before he'd gone up to Oxford, where his athletic skills had stood him in good stead, as the engraved oar proudly mounted on the grand landing of the Hall proclaimed. And the last time had been ... when?

She allowed her gaze to rest on him impersonally. She might recognise him, but there was no way he would know who she was. There had never been a reason why he should! It must have been all of eight years ago...

'Stay, boy!' Beneath her authoritative hand Sherlock ceased his growling, but he still guarded her, expectant, ready to move on a word of command.

Yes, she would have been fourteen. An unlovely, ungainly teenager who'd blushed when she'd been spoken to, content to watch her hero from afar. And what a hero! At twenty-three Luc Benchard could have reached out and plucked her for his own as easily as he'd helped himself to the ripe victoria plums in the orchard—only, of course, he hadn't even noticed her existence, and if he had how he would have mocked her devotion! For hadn't he had the pick of nearly every nubile girl in the vicinity?

Now she was older and mature enough to be able to judge a man on what he did rather than his appearance. Whatever Luc Benchard looked like now, she knew that nothing he could do or say would raise him in her estimation—not after the way he had ignored Amélie during the last year of her life!

'Don't mind the dog.' Her cool blue eyes offered him no welcome. 'He won't touch you unless I give the order.'

'That's gratifying news.' There was a smile in the deep voice that had once made her toes curl with delight. 'I didn't mean to startle you. I've been ringing the doorbell up at the house for the past ten minutes without avail, and then I remembered it's possible to climb over the shrubbery wall—with a bit of luck!' He gave a rueful laugh, bending slightly to rub his knees with the palm of his hand. 'I guess I was a bit rusty but I managed it at the third go.'

'So what was so urgent you had to go to the pains of trespassing?' She forbore to smile, unwilling to make him welcome when he had stayed away too long. Neither would she pay him the compliment, yet, of letting him know she had recognised him. He didn't deserve that either.

'I've come to see Amélie—Amélie Benchard...' Something about her stillness must have warned him because he paused and his voice became strained. 'Is something wrong?'

Two strides and he was directly in front of her, too close for comfort as she hesitated. Now she could clearly see every feature of his beautiful boyish face...only it wasn't beautiful or boyish any longer.

It was leaner than she remembered, the bones carved and chiselled to the fineness of an Aztec engraving, the cheeks hollowed beneath the flaring cheekbones, and only the jaw with its disarmingly rounded chin, the lustrous black hair on his head and the brilliant dark eyes that had once filled her dreams with nameless longings were the same.

'And who the devil are *you* anyway, and what are you doing on my grandmother's property?' There was anger in the fingers that reached for her shoulder as, with an arrogance typical of his approach to life, he ignored Sherlock's resumed growl. The kind of anger which conceals guilt? Her resolve strengthened. She would give it to him straight, without the gentle preparation she would have accorded a less selfish individual.

'I'm Aphra Grantly. I used to be Amélie's companion. Now I look after the property for the trustees of her estate.'

'Trustees?' Shock was reflected in the darkness of his eyes. 'You mean something has happened to Grand-mère Amélie? She can no longer manage her own affairs?' There was no mistaking the shock and dismay which contorted the clean lines of his face.

For a moment Aphra's wayward heart lurched in compassion, then she reminded herself that Luc Benchard's callous disregard of his grandmother's feelings had caused the lady much distress. Not that

Amélie had openly criticised him, but Aphra had grown close enough to her to realise the gnawing sadness her elderly employer had sustained.

'She died four weeks ago,' she told him expressionlessly, masking her own emotion. 'She'd already suffered one stroke several months ago, from which she'd appeared to make an almost complete recovery. Then, at the end of last month she suffered another one. The hospital did everything they could, but she had no fight left in her. She died within forty-eight hours.'

'Dear God!' Luc's voice was painfully constricted. 'She always seemed so strong. I had no idea...' His voice tailed away, but his expression left no need for words.

'Really?' Aphra returned evenly. 'I assumed you'd come here in response to one of the advertisements Amélie's solicitors placed asking you to contact them.' She paused briefly, wanting to give him no quarter but unable to ignore the signs of real distress on his personable face. 'Of course,' she continued coolly, 'if you'd kept in touch with her or left a forwarding address naturally you would have been informed, but since you chose to disappear out of her life completely...' She offered him an indifferent shrug.

'So—you do know who I am.' He pounced on her words with the speed of a feral cat sighting a mouse.

Again she made a slight movement with her shoulders, unwilling to pander to his inflated ego. 'I deduced your identity. After all, you called

Amélie Grand-mère, and to my certain knowledge she only had one grandson.'

She should have held her tongue at that stage, but the indignation which his silent absence had engendered over the past months of her employment had festered in the few weeks since Amélie's death, so that the words of recrimination tumbled from her lips.

'I don't think there was one day that she didn't talk about you; tell me the things you used to do, the honours you gained at school and college, how proud she was of you...' She swallowed down a rush of emotion.

This was no time to get sentimental, not when she was determined to let this arrogant playboy know exactly what she thought about his selfish disregard of the elderly woman who had become her friend. 'It wouldn't have cost you much to send her just one letter at Christmas or her birthday, would it?'

'What I did or didn't do is hardly your business, is it?' There was no mistaking the slight edge to his deep voice. 'But, for your information, I haven't seen any advertisements. I've come here directly from Heathrow.' His tone was grim. 'And I don't intend to stand out here much longer waiting for the rain to begin again.'

'I'll show you to the gate, then,' Aphra responded sweetly. 'Unless you intend leaving the way you entered?'

'I don't damn well intend leaving at all.' He shot her a furious glance. 'Since you know I'm Luc

Benchard, you also know I have every right to be here.'

'There's no need to raise your voice to me.' Aphra tossed her head, feeling the long plait into which she'd bound her pale blonde hair bounce against her shoulderblades. 'I've already told you that *I'm* in charge of the Hall with the blessing of the trustees until such time as the true heir is established. Until then, if anyone comes over that threshold it's at my invitation only. Is that clear?'

'Oh, it's clear enough, Miss Grantly, although without Cerberus here to lend you the help of his fangs I warrant you'd be hard put to enforce that decision.' He allowed his dark eyes to drift over her appraisingly with the air of someone summing up a troublesome opponent. There was nothing complimentary in his scrutiny. Nothing to suggest she was anything but an unmitigated nuisance.

'It's a large house with extensive grounds and I live here alone.' Her tone was cool, discouraging. 'Most of Mrs Benchard's valuables are in the bank, but the house is full of good furniture, which has to be protected. Sherlock is for its protection rather than mine.'

'Don't undersell yourself, Aphra.' For a fraction of a moment she was the recipient of the flashing, flirty smile that had once made her heart turn cartwheels. 'Your flesh and blood are infinitely more valuable than any wood and china and I'm sure Grand-mère would have agreed with me. You say you were her companion?' He raised thoughtful eyebrows. 'Your face does seem a little familiar.'

'Does it?' She returned his quizzical expression with a blank stare. 'But then there must have been a great number of blondes who have passed through your life. You're probably confusing me with someone else.'

'Perhaps.' There was a guarded impertinence in the look which raked over the high, firm breasts beneath her cotton shirt, before dropping to survey her neatly belted waist and, finally, to assess her long, shapely legs in the mud-soiled jeans which covered them. 'I admit I have no recollection of familiarity with your body.'

'At least in that respect your memory hasn't failed you!' She palmed her hands down the side of her denims, a sure sign of tension, and felt the pressure of her wedding ring against her thigh. 'I suggest you make an appointment with the solicitors who are acting as trustees. If you've got a pen and paper handy I'll give you their name and address—'

'And *I* suggest, Aphra, that you stop being provocative and invite me into my grandmother's house.' He eyed her steadily. 'Whatever my faults, I can assure you I don't attack women—even when they're not protected by large dogs. Quite apart from my moral integrity, I have no wish to be mauled by a ferocious hound! So be a good girl and take that hostile look off your face.'

He paused fractionally. 'I've come a long way, in the hope of being reunited with my grandmother, only to be greeted with the bald announcement of her death. Do you really expect me to turn tail and depart as if nothing has happened?'

His dark gaze scored down her face. 'Surely the least you can do is offer me a cup of coffee, if only as a tribute to Amélie's sense of hospitality?'

It was a hit below the belt because Aphra knew, however badly he'd neglected her, Amélie would have been overjoyed to welcome Luc back to Fairmead.

Besides, she admitted silently to herself, she must face up to reality. There was an outside chance she could deny Luc Benchard access to his inheritance today, but he only had to go to London, produce his marriage certificate for the executors' approval and Fairmead would be his forthwith. A fact of which he was perfectly well aware.

Her anger might be justified, but she was venturing on quicksands when she attempted to deny him his legal rights, and she'd little doubt that Luc Benchard would enjoy seeing her disappear beneath their sticky surface. She'd made her point. Reluctantly she accepted the fact that compromise was called for.

'Very well,' she said frigidly. 'I accept that Amélie would have made you welcome despite the heartache you caused her. In honour of her memory I'll do the same.' She slapped the dog lightly on his rump, said, 'Home, boy!' and watched as he shot off across the lawns towards the distant house.

'Ah, so you've decided to trust me after all.' Luc's face was still disturbingly drawn as he gazed down at her, satisfaction oozing from his voice. 'But perhaps it would be in both our interests if I showed you some identification. After all, it has been known for impostors to claim relationship in cases like this in order to ransack the property.' He raised a hand to his jacket but Aphra forestalled him.

'There's no need. I know you are Luc Benchard,' she said flatly, pausing slightly to give added impact to her next words. 'I always did.' Her blue eyes held his dark gaze, defying him to comment adversely on her attitude.

'Did you indeed?' He was as angry as she'd expected. 'So what's your problem, lady? Do I take it you're under the impression I did you some injury in the past? Is that why you are so bellicose? Or does your lack of a sympathetic and compassionate welcome reflect Grand-mère's last opinion of me?'

She'd started walking briskly towards the Hall, alarmingly aware of Luc's brooding presence at her side. Perhaps she'd been unwise to dismiss Sherlock so soon, she thought uneasily, although a whistle would bring him bounding back to her side...

'No, you don't!' Presumably reading her body language, Luc reached for her, swinging her round, one hand fastened determinedly on her shoulder. 'No woman makes dog's meat out of me! I want to know exactly what's going on. Did my father's dear cousin Leonard poison Grand-mère's mind against me whilst I was away? Did my lack of correspondence blacken me for ever in her eyes? Did she die hating me, Aphra? Is that it?'

His hand slackened slightly, but she sensed that any attempt to call Sherlock would be ruthlessly aborted. How dared he behave like this? To imagine that she'd once regarded this lout as a hero because of his prowess with the bat and the oar, the power of those long, beautifully muscled legs to carry him athletically over miles at a time without flagging, when the truth was that he was nothing but a whitened sepulchre—a beautiful exterior with a heart of dross.

No, Amélie had loved him to her last moment of consciousness. It was she, Aphra, who hated him on Amélie's behalf—a gratuitous, uncalled-for emotion which she'd never dared to voice, a feeling springing from her own friendship and respect for the proud and passionate Corsican woman who had become her friend as well as her employer. But she was in no mood to allay Luc's justified but unfulfilled fears so easily.

'You want to know if she cut you out of her will?' Scorn deepened the light blue of her eyes to pewter as she was filled with an uncharacteristic urge to strike him where she guessed it would hurt most. It was a need to avenge the fiery, lovable old lady he had ignored for so long—too long. 'No, she didn't.'

She watched his face begin to relax before adding, 'But the night before she had the second stroke she was very agitated, almost as if she knew that something was going to happen to her. She begged me to get in touch with her solicitor the next morning, insisting that she wanted to change her will. But by then, of course, it was too late.'

'Oh, dear God . . .' Luc groaned as his hand fell away from her arm, and a few drops of rain spattered down as she raised trembling fingers to touch the place where the heat of his flesh had burnt into hers.

'Yes, you seem to have been very lucky, Mr Benchard. All you have to do is produce your marriage certificate and my time as caretaker is over. I move out of Fairmead Hall as you and your wife move in!'

As the rain strengthened, she broke into a run, reaching the shelter of the elegant Georgian-style conservatory which stretched across the back of the house at the same time as Luc himself.

Wordlessly she unlocked the large double-glazed door, sliding it back, allowing him to enter. A tremor of unease shuddered down her spine as she walked across the marble-tiled floor, between the cretonne-cushioned cane furniture, towards the inner doors which would lead into the main part of the house. She wasn't at all sure she wanted to spend the night under the same roof as her fallen idol, but she could hardly expect him to move out of what was virtually his own home, could she? A fresh thought struck her. Pausing on the threshold, she turned to face him.

'Will your wife be joining you here tonight?'

'What wife, Aphra?' he snarled at her. 'What the hell do you think I've been doing with my life this last year? Spending it on a round-the-world honeymoon? Living it up in a vast round of pleasure, going from fashionable party to fashionable party, spending long nights of self-gratification with a beautiful and insatiable bride? Do you? Do you?' Fiercely he pinned her gaze, his dark eyes mesmerising her as she shrank back against the wall, stunned by his vehemence.

'How do I know what you've been doing?' She pulled herself together with an effort. In fact his angry description fitted very well with her imaginings, but now, she sensed, was not the time to admit it. 'All I was told was that you'd recently floated your electro-optical business on the Stock Exchange, not only making yourself very rich in the process but keeping enough shares to secure your future for many years ahead, and gone off to Venezuela with your fiancée. La bella Bellini, I think Amélie called her.'

'Kathryn Bellini, yes.' He moved his head in a sharp, acquiescent gesture. 'I expect Grand-mère also told you that she was a photographic model of great beauty and charisma?'

'Something like that,' Aphra agreed demurely, recalling Amélie's acrid description of her future granddaughter-in-law as 'an empty-headed, scrawny, *poseuse* who would bore Luc to death after the first throes of lust had been expended'. 'She felt nothing was more natural than that the two of you should take a year off to tour around South America. Obviously she knew you'd arranged for all your personal and business matters to be handled through your office while you were absent, but that didn't stop her eagerly waiting every visit from the postman, or help her hide her disappointment when month followed month and she heard nothing!'

'Was she worried about me?' he asked tightly.

'What do you think?' Aphra's small chin tilted belligerently. 'Oh, she pretended not to be ... said that you were probably enjoying yourself too much to send a postcard or make a phone call. She consoled herself with the thought that if you'd met with an accident the authorities would have been in touch, that if you'd been taken ill La Bella . . . that is . . .' swiftly she corrected herself '. . . your fiancée would have let her know.'

She drew in a steadying breath, too hyped up to respond to the still whiteness of Luc's face as she continued scathingly, 'So why did you treat her in such a cavalier fashion, not even a card or phone call on her birthday or at Christmas? This country isn't the only place which has pillar-boxes, is it? Or were you so occupied with winning your sports blues that you never got round to learning to write?'

'At least *I* was taught the art of polite conversation.' Something in his deep, harsh voice warned her that she was treading on dangerous ground when she dared to question his behaviour.

Perhaps her response had been too impertinent, yet he deserved to know how much his grandmother had suffered in his absence, and since Amélie wasn't here to tell him herself . . .

'Then it's a pity they didn't include lessons in the curriculum on how to treat with consideration the people who love you.' Despite his rebuke, she stood her ground, refusing to be cowed. Only she knew how much Amélie had suffered over the silence of the past year. Luc's behaviour had been despicable.

'It's not enough to look good, be clever and excel at sport.' She continued her lecture with quiet determination. 'But then perhaps you've never heard of the saying Manners maketh man?'

'Actually it was the motto of my public school,' he informed her coldly. 'Which is why I'm standing here at this moment attempting to keep my temper under control, when a less patient man would be reminding you with some vigour that it's not the duty of the housekeeper to lecture her master!'

Physical vigour, did he mean? There was a gleam in his dark eyes that cautioned her to silence, a glint that threatened her with retribution she might not enjoy!

Aphra passed her tongue over lips which had become suddenly dry as she decided that a little discretion on her part might be called for; but she wouldn't surrender her position without defending it one more time.

'Before I became the "housekeeper", as you choose to call it, I was Amélie's companion and friend. As far as I'm concerned, you're the grandson who caused her such distress towards the end of her life—certainly not my master, and you never will be! The moment you and your wife acquaint the solicitors of your presence in England, my duties come to an end.'

Fixing her proud face with a jaundiced eye, Luc flung himself down in one of the comfortable wicker chairs, stretching his legs out in front of him. 'Since you chose to ignore my previous question, Aphra Grantly, I'll repeat it. What wife?'

Aphra frowned, a frightening chasm of disbelief yawning in her mind. 'You mean you haven't married Kathryn Bellini?'

'Isn't that what I've just said?' he demanded shortly. 'She walked out on me shortly after we arrived in Venezuela. The next time I saw her was on the front cover of a women's magazine—with her new husband...Felipe Carreira, the Grand Prix driver.'

'Oh, I see.' Aphra stared at him blankly, seeing nothing. It was the last news she'd been expecting to hear. The handsome, rich, desirable Luc Benchard jilted? So much for her fantasy of his spending a prolonged honeymoon, too involved with his beautiful wife to spare a thought for the frail old lady he'd left behind in England—the grandmother who'd nursed and loved him as her own, after his parents had been killed outright in a cable-car disaster in the Alps when he'd been five years old. 'You must have done something pretty awful for her to have left you,' she added frankly, her imagination working overtime.

'Apparently Kathryn would agree with you.' A blank stare met the curiosity in her gaze.

'And you didn't replace her with anyone else?' It seemed impossible that he hadn't been surrounded by nubile women in Buenos Aires or Rio or Caracas...or wherever his wanderlust had taken him; and equally unlikely that there wouldn't have been at least one who would have filled the vacant place in his heart—and his bed.

'No, I didn't,' he growled, adding irritably, 'I've changed my mind about coffee. Is there anything alcoholic to drink in this house, or are you a teetotaller as well as a scold?'

'Will Scotch be OK?'

Assailed by sudden guilt at the way she'd broken the news of his grandmother's death to him, and at her subsequent inhospitality, Aphra accepted the rebuke without comment.

'Fine!' Luc dredged up an apology for a smile from somewhere, but it was apparent that weariness was fast overtaking him.

Aphra made her way to the drinks trolley where the various bottles had stood carefully dusted but unopened since Amélie's death, and found her hand shaking as she poured out a good measure into a lead-crystal tumbler.

'Water? Soda? Dry ginger?' Politely she invited his choice.

'As it comes—thanks.' He took the glass from her hand and swallowed a mouthful, before throwing his head back and closing his eyes, allowing the smooth single malt to work its magic.

Absently Aphra watched the movement of the larynx in his long throat, observed the lines of strain which turned the once boyish countenance into that of an experienced man.

It seemed that Kathryn's defection had hit him hard. Was it possible that he'd suffered some kind of deep trauma after she'd met and married another man, perhaps even gone on some kind of retreat from the world, shutting himself off from all communications? Was that why he hadn't been in touch with Amélie?

A vivid mental picture of him wearing chaps and a leather jacket and sitting astride a black stallion as he stared over a vast, treeless wilderness flickered across her mind. Quickly she dismissed it. Whatever his reasons for neglect, they were no longer relevant in view of the bombshell he had just dropped.

She took a deep breath, acknowledging that the way she'd received him was hardly likely to have endeared her to him. Most probably he wouldn't want to discuss his future with her, but loyalty to Amélie made it imperative she forced him to face the legal consequences of Kathryn's departure from his life.

'Luc...' she began tentatively. Then, when he showed no sign of having heard her, she dropped impulsively to her knees at his feet, peering into his relaxed face, resting her palms on one of his long thighs in an effort to gain his attention. 'Luc—the Hall. If you're not married, what is going to happen to Fairmead Hall?'

CHAPTER TWO

'WHATEVER my grandmother wished to happen to it, presumably.' A quick glance down at where her hands rested on the dark material which covered his legs brought the colour flaring to Aphra's cheeks as speedily she withdrew the offending fingers.

How could Luc be so casual about the beautiful house—no, *home*—where his own father had been raised and where he'd spent so much of his own youth? She felt like shaking him!

'Amélie told me the terms of her will,' she continued doggedly, 'and the reason she imposed them ten years ago. She said she didn't want you to miss out on the joys of a permanent relationship, the trials and pleasures of having your own family.

'She said she'd been denied the joy of growing old with the man she loved when your grandfather was killed during the Second World War, that her son, your own father, Robert, was cheated when he and your devoted mother were killed in an accident when you were barely five years old...'

'You've been well briefed.' Did she fancy his lip curled superciliously as a slight dip of his sable head acknowledged the sad truths, encouraging her to continue?

'She said it was her dearest wish that you, her sole blood relative, should inherit the happiness that had passed all the other Benchards by.' She pursued her argument, unhappily aware of his impatient regard but determined to have her say. 'So she deliberately made the condition that you should inherit Fairmead on her death, but only if you were married before your thirty-first birthday. In the event of her death before that time the Hall was to be held in trust and, failing your complying with her wishes, everything was to go to her nephew-in-law, Leonard.' His silence confused her, so that she added rather sharply, 'She told me you were perfectly aware of the terms.'

'Yes, I was and I am. I wish Leonard well of it.' Luc tossed back the remainder of the Scotch. 'And now, if I'm to drive back to the nearest town and find a room for the night before going back to London, I'd better go or I'll fall asleep at the wheel.'

'But you just can't go like that, as if it's not important!' Distraught, Aphra jumped to her feet and stood barring his path, her eyes flashing fire. 'You know as well as I do that Amélie detested Leonard, that your grandfather's brother made Amélie's life hell here when she arrived as a teenage bride unable to speak a word of English! He mocked and humiliated her, treated her as an imbecile because she didn't even speak Parisian French—'

'She didn't speak French at all.' Luc's lips twisted in a wry smile. 'She spoke a Corsican patois. My grandfather's family regarded her as a savage and did everything they could to force her to pack her bags and return to her "God-forsaken island", as they called it. But she was made of sterner stuff; besides, she truly loved my grandfather, so she stuck it out.'

Aphra made an impatient gesture with her hands, wishing she could shake Luc into some kind of action. 'Exactly! And apparently almost from the day he was born Leonard was schooled to treat his aunt with similar disrespect and contempt,' she contributed acidly. 'Surely you're aware your grandmother *deliberately* named Leonard as her heir in default of your marrying because she knew you shared her feelings about him and she believed it the most powerful weapon she could use to stimulate you to settle down?'

'So, she miscalculated.' He rose to his feet. 'Moral blackmail is a dangerous game to play.'

'No, Luc, please!' It was as if by some strange metamorphosis she'd been endowed with Amélie's fighting spirit, the doggedness which would not submit whilst there was one atom of chance left for her to gain her own ends. 'Despite everything that's happened, this is still your home,' she continued, astonished by the sense of desperation which flooded through her body. 'At least stay the night here. All the rooms are aired and bed-linen's no problem. I can make you up a room in ten minutes!' Only a short while ago she'd wanted him to leave; now it was as if her whole purpose in life depended on his staying.

'To what purpose?' With eyes empty of expression he looked into her earnest face. 'There's nothing here for me now.'

'But there must be something you can do,' she persevered, suppressing a sudden shiver which trembled down her spine as Sherlock, lying relaxed just inside the door, lifted his beautiful head and growled softly in his throat. 'How can you possibly give up so easily when so much is at stake? I know you're not thirty-one for another two weeks. Amélie told me. As the time went by and she heard nothing from you, she became more and more fretful.

'She said she knew you so well, that she was sure you wouldn't let her down, that you and La B—' again she abandoned Amélie's contemptuous nickname for the svelte model who had captured her grandson's heart '—you and Kathryn Bellini must already be man and wife. After all, you'd been engaged for over six months when you arranged your South American holiday, and you knew the terms of her will.'

Her voice softened, became sad with remembrance. 'She used to mark the days off on her calendar, waiting for the confirmation of her hopes, and all the time she was becoming more and more agitated.'

'With good cause,' Luc said drily, his eyes expressionless.

'But does it have to be like this?' Roughly Aphra challenged him. 'It's still in your power to make the deadline and fulfil the terms—'

'And how do I go about that?' He was laughing at her—the first genuine amusement she'd seen on his face that evening. 'Charm some nubile female down from the trees?'

'You always used to...' The words were out before she'd considered their wisdom.

'I *do* know you.' His hand reached out, more gently this time, and took her chin lightly. Eyes as black as night sought inspiration from her innocent blue gaze as she held her breath. Then he shook his head. 'Well, no matter. It'll come to me.'

'There must be some woman in your life,' she persisted obstinately. 'Some girl of whom you're fond and who would accept a proposal from you?'

'No.' He met her challenge with a slight shake of his head. 'There's been no one since Kathryn.'

'Then perhaps you could find someone who would come to some arrangement with you, marry you in return for British citizenship or an agreed payment, or something like that?' she went on doggedly, painfully aware of the bitterness behind his denial.

'Possibly.' He shrugged, a hint of amusement gleaming in the depth of his eyes. 'We live in a commercial world. There's a market for everything. But what you suggest is not only illegal but could leave me open to all kinds of blackmail, quite apart from the fact that I happen to be very fussy about the women I take into my bed.' He paused slightly. 'Besides which, there's one important thing you've overlooked.'

'What?' Anxiously her long-lashed eyes surveyed the stillness of his face as he drew in a steady breath. 'I have no desire to inherit Fairmead Hall.'

'But you must!' The pitch of Aphra's voice rose in anguish. 'It's so beautiful and you spent your childhood here. Even when you were up at university you spent the long vacation here—'

'That was in the past,' he interrupted curtly. 'And, like my grandmother—the past is dead.'

'So you intend to surrender your birthright without even considering a way of keeping it?'

Contemptuously Aphra lifted her head to cast her scathing regard across his brooding face. 'Strange, but I never thought of you as shirking responsibility.'

'And I never thought I should have to deal with a shrill-voiced shrew in the same hour as being informed of a painful bereavement!' His voice was like a slap, hard, devoid of any emotion but outrage.

Aphra swallowed, a wave of shame engulfing her at his harsh stricture. Perhaps she had raised her voice more than was necessary, but 'shrew' was a painful epithet to digest when all she'd been doing was trying to fight for what her dear friend had wanted ... had reiterated with what, in retrospect, had been her last coherent breath.

Making a conscious effort to soften her tone, she kept her gaze fixed to Luc's accusing countenance. 'I apologise if my manner has offended you,' she said stiffly, 'but I feel I owe it to your grandmother to argue her case since she's unable to speak for herself.

'It was more than a whim. It was her life's ambition that her Corsican blood should run through generation after generation of the Benchard clan, because she herself had had to fight so hard for the recognition she'd deserved. In the early 1930s when she came here as a young bride there was so much snobbishness, class awareness ...' Her eyes pleaded with him as her voice broke emotionally.

'I know the story.' He made a dismissive gesture with one hand. 'Even without your graphic and poignant reiteration of it.'

'Then if you haven't forgotten—'

'I've forgotten nothing,' he interrupted her impatiently. 'But you have.'

He thrust his hands deep down into his trouser pockets, bracing his legs and staring out across her head to where the rain lashed down mercilessly against the glass walls of the conservatory. 'Even if by some miracle I could fulfil the terms of Grandmère's will and find myself a compatible female who'd be prepared to endure a loveless marriage in exchange for financial well-being, Amélie still, according to you, wanted to change her will.'

His eyes smouldered with a deep-burning fire as he drew in a deep breath, returning his gaze to her questioning face. 'Do you really think I would want the Hall, knowing she no longer cared for or trusted me? That in her opinion I'd betrayed her and all she stood for? That she no longer wanted me here? Do you, Aphra?'

'Oh!' His caustic tone brought a guilty flush to her pale skin as she recalled the deliberately evasive way she'd informed him of Amélie's change of heart. There was no help for it. She would have to confess what had really happened. She drew in a deep breath. 'I'm afraid I may have inadvertently misled you about that,' she offered diffidently.

'You mean you were lying when you told me that her last wish was to change her will?' Luc's voice grated ominously, commanding her full attention.

'No, no...' Quickly she rushed to defend herself. 'It was true that she wanted to change it. As the days went past and the deadline drew nearer without a word from you, she began to wonder if you might, after all, choose to defy her wishes because you shared her own indomitable pride and resented being manipulated.'

For a moment Aphra glanced away, unable to bear the intensity of Luc's appraisal, before bravely forcing her eyes back to meet the bleakness of his gaze as she told him the unvarnished truth. 'Yes, she decided to change her will. She wanted to revoke what she knew to be an unfair and contentious requirement. Your grandmother wanted to leave Fairmead Hall to you absolutely and entirely without any conditions whatsoever. That was what she intended to tell her solicitor.'

'I see.' Luc expelled his breath in a long sigh. 'Well, at least it's some comfort to know that she didn't die cursing me.' He moved his shoulders wearily as if a burden had been lifted from them. 'In the circumstances I think I will accept your offer of a bed for the night.'

She'd won a small battle but common sense told her the war had been lost. A few hours later Aphra climbed wearily into her own comfortable bed, forsaking her usual custom of reading, to lie in the darkness, turning over the events of the evening in her mind.

Not only had she prepared what she knew to be Luc's old room for him, but she'd produced a meal, using some of the basic contents of the freezer to create a tasty bolognese sauce to accompany a plateful of spaghetti. At his request she'd joined him at the table, finding she had little appetite but making a pretence of enjoying the food. As if by mutual consent there had been little conversation.

To be truthful, she'd begun to feel ashamed of the way in which she'd greeted him. She'd had no right to take him to task for neglecting Amélie. She was an outsider, an onlooker, and although, proverbially, such people saw most of the game the manner in which she'd broken the news of his grandmother's death had been impertinent and heartless.

Watching him surreptitiously from beneath her lowered lashes as he'd dealt competently with the long strands of pasta, winding them neatly around his fork, she'd sensed his inner pain, the aching loss of bereavement tamped down by the rigid self-control that adult Anglo-Saxons were expected to apply to their wayward emotions. Yet Luc Benchard had inherited a powerful dose of Amélie's vibrant Mediterranean spirit along with her dramatic colouring, and the battle for control must have been a painful one.

Also she'd been embarrassed. In retrospect her angry suggestion that Luc should find himself a wife for the sole purpose of inheriting the Hall had been ridiculous. Unconsciously she twisted the gold ring on her own finger, remembering the expression on Peter's face when he'd begged her to become his wife. Love might not be the only valid reason for marrying—dynasties were founded, ancient bloodlines amalgamated for a title, and beauty offered for social position and wealth—but no man in his right senses could be expected to invite a stranger into his life for the sole purpose of fulfilling the terms of a will which should never have been made.

Damn Kathryn Bellini! she thought uncharitably. Luc Benchard had more than his fair share of sterling qualities and he was handsome and wealthy to boot! Also he'd obviously loved the wretched woman to desperation. That much was obvious from his demeanour. What more had she wanted?

Sleep came to her late and sporadically, so that when the first light of morning pierced the curtains Aphra was only too glad to get up and start the day; her first duty being to take Sherlock for his morning run in the nearby country park.

Well-behaved and obedient, he could safely be let off his leash where regulations permitted it. Always she enjoyed jogging along in his wake, but this morning her normally controlled pace had somehow turned into something more like a sprint, so that by the time she arrived back at the Hall she was flushed and panting, tendrils of blonde hair, dislodged from their controlling plait, clinging to her face and neck.

Entering the house through the conservatory, she was greeted by the welcoming scent of freshly brewed coffee. Following it to its source, she found Luc perched on one of the stools in the country-style kitchen, its south-eastern aspect already reflecting the misty warmth of the morning.

Shaved and wearing a close-fitting white cotton shirt which emphasised the deep golden tan of his arms, he acknowledged her entrance with a swift, speculative glance which encompassed every inch

of her, from the glowing pink skin of her face, past
the baggy blue T-shirt and navy tracksuit bottoms
to her trainer-clad feet.

'I've made myself at home,' he commented drily.
'I take it you have no objections?'

'Of course not.' She accepted the glass of orange
juice he poured for her. 'This is your home.' She
took a long, grateful swallow of the cold liquid
before adding, 'Temporarily.' Immediately she
could have bitten her tongue. Where had all her
resolutions of the previous evening disappeared to?
What was there about this man which drove her to
taunt him?

'Indeed.' Calmly he accepted her qualification.
'So I mean to make the most of it for the few days
remaining to me. However, as far as the trustees
are concerned, I've decided to tell them I shall be
fulfilling the terms of Grand-mère's will before the
deadline.' He sipped reflectively at the liquid in his
mug. 'That ought to make Leonard sweat a little.
Coffee?'

'Not as much as he deserves.' Aphra nodded her
acceptance of his offer, taking up her position on
the remaining stool beside the breakfast bar, adding
impulsively, 'Oh, why did events have to turn out
like this? I'm so sorry, Luc! You must love
Fairmead Hall even more than I do! How can you
bear to think of Leonard living here, destroying
every memory of Amélie, obliterating every trace
of her taste—?'

'I can't,' he interrupted her calmly. 'But, fortunately, I don't see that happening. When Leonard
inherits the Hall he'll also be liable for the in-

heritance tax which goes with it. There's no way
he'll be able to pay that. His only option will be to
put it up for sale, and meet the tax from the
proceeds.'

'Of course; why didn't I think of that?' Aphra
exclaimed delightedly, a great wave of relief washing
over her. 'You'll be able to buy it from him, so
Amélie will get her wish after all...' Her voice
faltered to a stop, her heart plummeting as she read
the denial on his face. 'Won't you?' she asked
shakily.

'You think he'd entertain the idea of me as a
buyer for one moment?' His slightly raised eyebrows mocked her naïvety. 'Since *Grand-mère's* told
you so much about our family you must know that
the feud which exists between us is as deep and
powerful as the Corsican vendetta itself, the blood
feud of her native country. No,' he continued, his
voice resigned, 'Leonard would never sell to me or
to anyone he suspected of being my representative.
Knowing him, I imagine he already has a buyer in
mind. All I can do is hope that its new owner will
love and care for it as much as Amélie would desire.'

'Or spend the morning going through your address book?' It had been meant as a joke. Last night
she'd seen reason, hadn't she? She'd abandoned any
hope of his producing a potential wife from his
eventful past; so why did the words proceed from
her lips with the hopeful intonation of a question?

Briskly she rose to her feet, indicating she expected no answer to her wayward comment. 'I'm
sure you usually eat more for breakfast than juice
and coffee,' she said hurriedly. 'How about I cook

you a good old English breakfast—eggs, bacon, fried bread—?'

'What is it with you, Aphra?' He'd moved lazily from the stool to tower above her. 'I accept you cared for my grandmother, and I loved her too, more than you can possibly appreciate. It couldn't have been easy for her to recover from the tragedy of her only son's death and find herself with the responsibility of bringing up an orphaned five-year-old, but she brought warmth and colour and her own *joie de vivre* into my life, so that I never felt emotionally deprived.' He sighed an impatient breath as he struck one fist into the palm of his other hand, his deep voice harshening. 'But some sacrifices are too dear to make for any cause. True, Amélie wouldn't have wanted the Hall sold outside the family, but even less would she have wanted me to tie myself to a life of bitterness and unfulfilment, or leave myself open to blackmail or a lifetime of legal wrangles.'

'Yes, I understand.' Aphra's heart was pounding to the rhythm of the tumble-drier she could hear operating in the background. Luc must have done some washing, she thought distractedly, remembering the small holdall which had been his only luggage. 'I'll get you some break—' She'd started towards the fridge, only to stop speaking as Luc intercepted her passage, taking her firmly by the arms and forcing her to a standstill.

'What do you understand, Aphra?' he asked gently—too gently. 'What deep inner knowledge do you have about living intimately with another human being? Where, for instance, does *Mr* Grantly figure in your life?'

One hand had lowered to seize her left hand, lifting it to his chest level, forcing her by sheer will-power to cast her eyes down to the ring which encircled her third finger.

He was close—too close—and all the memories and dreams of her lonely adolescence revived to torment her. Some dormant emotion, long since crushed into submission, rose like a phoenix in her being, so that it was all she could do not to close her eyes and lean towards him, inviting the warm, persuasive power of his mouth to ease away the pain of her loneliness.

Peter. How could she explain her relationship with Peter to this vibrant, healthy male whose pores oozed mental and physical well-being? She'd been eighteen when she'd met Peter, twenty-one when she'd married him, knowing he was dying, and still twenty-one when she'd become a widow. The memory was too raw to air before the man whose appearance had reawakened the romantic dreams of her youth. Pity from Luc would be intolerable. But she had to give him an answer. The warmth of his fingers tightening around her hand demanded it, and she wouldn't lie.

'It didn't work out,' she told him, raising her chin defiantly to stare unrepentingly into his darkly questioning gaze. 'We're no longer together.'

'Hmm! Fools rush in. Was that it, Aphra?' She'd hoped that her explanation would persuade him to relinquish her hand but he seemed in no hurry to do so. 'A teenage romance, was it?'

She didn't deny it. 'We met at the college where I was training to become a speech therapist.'

His dark eyebrows rose. 'And you fell so madly in love with him that you gave up your training to marry him?'

Stung by the implied contempt in the question, she wrenched her hand away from his grasp. 'On the contrary, I passed my final exams with honours.'

'But decided that becoming a companion to an elderly lady might prove a more *rewarding* and a less onerous calling?'

'You think I was expecting Amélie to leave me something in her will?' Astounded by his implication, she found herself shaking with anger. 'I came back here to Leamarsh to recuperate emotionally after—' Hastily she readjusted her thoughts. She'd been about to say 'after Peter's death', but her reasons for concealing his fate had increased a hundredfold since Luc's bitter accusation. 'After my marriage ended,' she substituted coldly. 'If you'd been around at the time you would have been aware that your grandmother had recently returned to the Hall after being discharged from the local hospital following partial recovery from her first stroke.'

She took pleasure from seeing the shadow which crossed his face before continuing adamantly, 'Yes, she needed a companion, but I could offer her more than that. You see, she was suffering from aphasia—the inability to form words correctly—as a direct consequence of her illness. I could give her expert help to encourage her to speak coherently once again.'

Her head came up proudly. Incensed at the injustice of his accusation, she stared him boldly in the eye. 'If you can remember what your grandmother was like when last you saw her, you'll recall the delight she took in argument and discussion. I thought I could help her regain that faculty—and I did! If there was anything mean or underhand in that, then I plead guilty to it.' She inhaled a deep, refreshing breath into her adrenalin-charged system. 'Now, do you want a cooked breakfast or not?'

'Not, I think.' Luc regarded her enraged face with what, to her chagrin, appeared to be a hint of humour lurking behind his brilliant eyes. 'Since, if it contained mushrooms, I'd have very grave doubts about the wisdom of consuming it.'

'You're accusing me of murderous intentions now?' She regarded him balefully. 'Believe me, I value my freedom too dearly to risk it for the momentary satisfaction of exacting vengeance on an ill-informed itinerant.'

Despite her very real hurt, she felt her lips begin to curl as she realised how ridiculous the two of them would appear to an onlooker. 'Besides,' she added sweetly, 'I'm quite prepared to accept an apology for your rudeness.'

She hadn't known what to expect from him, but it certainly wasn't the long, contemplative scrutiny to which she was being subjected.

'"Back to Leamarsh..."' he was muttering. '"Prepared to accept an apology for your rudeness—"'

She stirred uncomfortably, beginning to ease her way towards the kitchen door as memories she would rather have consigned to oblivion flashed in quick succession across the screen of her mind. She was just reaching out thankfully to pull it open when behind her she heard Luc's crow of delight.

'Got it! I remember you now. You're Annie. Little Annie Glover!'

CHAPTER THREE

APHRA froze. How could Luc possibly recognise her or remember what she'd been called by her playmates all those years ago, when, desperate to make friends with the summer visitors on the new caravan site, she'd introduced herself as Annie, rather than leave herself open to taunts about her unusual name?

Reluctantly she turned to face him, her heart sinking as she saw from the malicious gleam in his dark eyes that his memory had delivered—and in trumps!

'Well, well, little Annie Glover,' he repeated. 'The girl who caused my first serious romance to come to an abrupt end when she called Marilyn Rogers a stupid, smelly townee.'

'Yes, well...' Colour flushed her cheeks as she remembered the angry confrontation in the country lane. 'I admit I was very rude—'

'Oh, you were, darling, you were.' Luc reinforced her own retrospective opinion with relish. 'In fact Marilyn was all for reporting your lack of manners to your redoubtable aunt with a call for suitable chastisement.'

'I was only eight years old at the time if I remember correctly. It's an age when children take things deeply to heart.'

Even so, now, many years later, she felt forced to offer her explanation. 'When I saw that silly girl billing and cooing over that poor little lamb all I could think of was that, with her scent all over it, its mother would never accept it again and it would be left all alone to die.'

'Mmm, I remember your logic, but it wasn't the most tactful way to express yourself—ordering her to put it down before she made it smell as horrible as she did.'

'She did smell horrible,' Aphra shrugged, unrepentant. 'I've never liked perfumes with a heavy musk undertone. It smelt like she needed a bath—and I'm sure the lamb hated it.'

'He certainly gambolled away at full speed the moment she released him,' Luc agreed pleasantly enough. 'Unfortunately, in his haste to rejoin his mother before she forgot who he was, he managed to rip the buttons from Marilyn's blouse. Her face was a picture, and I'm afraid she didn't appreciate my laughing.'

'So that's why she dumped you, is it?' she asked curiously, remembering with a smug sense of satisfaction how pleased she'd been when the over-made-up Marilyn had disappeared from the social scene. 'Well, if you want my opinion it was no big deal. Who wants a girlfriend without a sense of humour—or a sense of smell, for that matter?'

'A young man who wants to impress his peers by being seen with a beautiful woman?' Luc raised interrogative eyebrows.

'Huh!' She dismissed the suggestion with scant regard. 'You had enough trophies to impress a legion of your contemporaries. One silly, simpering girl who knew nothing better than to walk through fields wearing high heels and assaulting the livestock would hardly have added to your status.'

'Jealous, Annie, were you?' Luc asked softly, eyes narrowed as they dwelt on her quarrelsome-looking face. 'Did you want me for yourself?'

'At eight years of age?' Her voice rose in indignation. 'If you must know, I thought you were as stupid as Marilyn. You should never have allowed her to pick the lamb up in the first place. You were country born and raised. You must have known its mother could reject it if she didn't recognise its scent.'

Not a lie. At eight she hadn't harboured any feelings towards him, she consoled herself. Those had come later, when childhood had developed into adolescence, and she'd undergone the first throes of a painful yet delightful hero-worship.

'But then I had plans for Marilyn,' he told her easily. 'And they didn't include offending her.'

Aphra shrugged. 'If a burst of laughter offended her, then she might have been even more offended by the plans you had in store for her. Perhaps you both had a lucky escape?'

'Perhaps.' He didn't sound too sure, and she guessed he was recalling the ache of unrequited love which must have torn his virile, youthful body at Marilyn's abrupt departure from his life. 'But it wasn't just my mirth to which she objected. It was my refusal to march straight down to Auntie Glover to demand that a suitable and painful punishment be inflicted on you without delay.'

'Dear Auntie Glover!' Aphra smiled, wondering what Luc would say if she told him the truth—that 'Auntie' Glover had been no relation to her at all, but her father's old nanny, brought out of retirement to take her to their rented cottage in Leamarsh and care for her during the long summer holidays from boarding-school.

'She was the prototype for the saying about someone's bark being worse than their bite,' she continued reminiscently. 'Believe me, she looked a lot more fierce than she was. Actually I think she would have agreed with my stand against cruelty to animals.'

'But not condoned the impertinent tone you used to declare it, surely?'

'Is it important—all these years later?'

'It could be.' Luc nodded. 'Let's just say it's a debt still to be paid, Annie.'

She laughed. 'My name's Aphra.'

'Changed it by deed poll to sound more glamorous, did you?'

Was this what he'd meant by collecting a debt—using this irritating tone of voice to wind her up? Certainly, ever since he'd recalled that long-ago encounter, the friction between them had increased. She could feel it like an electric presence, tingling and sparking, innately dangerous.

'I was christened Aphra, but the other children used to make fun of it,' she informed him stiffly. The culprits had not been her contemporaries at the expensive boarding-school to which she'd been sent whilst her parents were away in the Middle Eastern oil states, but the 'ordinary' children—the ones who played rounders on the newly established summer caravan site in the village and hide-and-seek in the surrounding woods. The ones whose gangs she'd wanted to join. 'So I told them my name was Annie.'

The same explanation applied to her reason for letting the children believe 'Auntie' Glover had been her real aunt—her father's sister. Even at that tender age she'd learned that Beaumont-Valance was not a name to be absorbed without comment by the cheerful, friendly crowd brought by charitable associations from the inner London boroughs to enjoy the fresh country air.

'Aphra...' Luc mused. 'Short for Aphrodite, is it?'

'Who knows? My mother chose it. She thought it sounded pretty. But my father once told me that it had a Biblical connotation, that Aphrah was referred to by one of the prophets as the "House of Dust".'

Luc's eyebrows shot up. 'Amazing! A less dusty person I have yet to meet! Personally I prefer to think of it as an abbreviation for Aphrodite.'

He tilted his head slightly to one side as he scrutinised her carefully. 'Come to think of it, you do bear a resemblance to a painting I once saw of the Greek goddess of love. Of course, she wasn't wearing tracksuit bottoms or trainers... In fact, if I remember correctly, she wasn't wearing anything at all, but the hair was the same... At least it would have been if you disengaged that childish plait...'

He moved towards her and she reared back against

the door, her hands rising to protect her threatened hairdo.

'Keep your hands off me, Luc Benchard,' she breathed. 'Or I'll set Sherlock on you.'

'No, you won't, Aphra Grantly.' He was so close to her that she felt overwhelmed by his sheer physical presence, relentless images of his splendid male body clothed in the emotive uniforms of sport flashing across her memory. What wouldn't she have given at fourteen to be in such proximity to the dashing hero of her dreams? 'Because,' he was continuing softly, 'you're a fair-minded girl. You believe in justice and obedience, don't you?'

He wasn't expecting an answer, and she was in no mind to give him one. To deny his assertion would be false. To admit to it would be madness. Instead she turned her head, so that her cheek pressed against the cool wood of the door. Out of the corner of her eye she espied Sherlock, still patiently waiting to be fed, sitting erectly expectant, panting in a rhythm that seemed to echo her own rapid expellation of breath.

'So,' Luc went on in the tone of voice one would use to a particularly dense child, 'you won't be surprised when I tell you I intend to collect the first instalment on the debt you owe me for throwing a spanner into my plans for a splendid summer weekend.'

Unable to meet the brilliant, seductive gaze he lavished on her, Aphra closed her eyes. 'Fourteen years,' she murmured distractedly. 'It must be all of fourteen years ago.'

'A long time for the interest to accumulate, hmm?'

His mouth found hers at the same time as his hands slid round her body, easing her away from the door with the same delicate, powerful skill which had marked his prowess on the sports field.

Playboy! Inconsiderate grandson! If she had opposed him he would have released her, but opposition was the furthest thought from her mind. Magically time seemed to have turned full circle and she was a young, gauche teenager again, reliving her romantic dreams, exalting in the imagined glory of being loved by Luc Benchard.

Instinctively her hands rose to trace the hard line of his spine, pulling his body closer to her own, moving possessively down the firm muscles of his back, her hands lacing against the taut, hard curve of his loins as she drew him into the cradle of her own pelvis.

Feeling his body grow tense against her, she knew one great joyous flare of triumph on behalf of little Annie Glover, then reality closed in on her and she was fighting for her release, stiffening and twisting in his embrace as shame replaced the euphoria of achievement.

Her intention had been to exorcise the ghosts of the past. Far from succeeding, to her deep despair and humiliation she realised with horror that she'd succeeded in stirring the dormant innocent fantasies of her youth to uneasy wakefulness.

To his credit Luc released her instantly, taking a step backwards, as instinctively her hands rose to her lips as if to deny she had been a willing participant in what had occurred.

Her eyes sliding away from his too-encompassing gaze, she fought to regain her composure, to limit the damage she must have done to her image in his eyes.

'Now perhaps we can consider my childhood debt settled once and for all and leave the incident where it belongs—in the past,' she muttered angrily.

'Why not?' Luc's wickedly seductive mouth twisted, a flash of sarcasm gleaming in the depth of his eyes as they dwelt on her pinkened cheeks. 'When a minor peccadillo has been so charmingly and enthusiastically paid for, only a usurer would demand more.' He paused thoughtfully as she tensed herself in preparation for some snide comment, only to add lightly, 'Do you know, I think I'll have that cooked breakfast after all? I'll be in the conservatory when it's ready.'

She stepped aside, allowing him to leave the room, thankful that he hadn't attempted further intimacies in order to embarrass her. How could she have been so stupid? Shivering at her own loss of control, she began methodically to assemble the food she needed.

She'd always enjoyed the preparation and cooking of food; the working to a final end which could be perceived and enjoyed. It had been the same with the therapy she'd studied—the challenge of working towards a steady improvement.

Going through the ritual of cooking the great British breakfast, she thought back to her early days at college, her burning desire to work with verbally challenged children, to ease their frustration and enable them to communicate on equal terms with their friends and families.

She had been fired with ambition based on the deep need to be of some service to others ... and Peter had shared her enthusiasm. They'd been friends, physically close but not intimate because they'd both been idealists; wanting to wait until they were sure of their lifelong commitment to each other before becoming lovers in the deepest sense of the word.

Lifelong commitment! Her jaws clenching to control the onset of tears, Aphra flipped over the eggs in the pan before her. Peter had been twenty-two years of age when he'd died of leukaemia, peacefully in hospital, two days after their wedding. And she had been at his side.

After that, all she'd wanted was to escape from the condolences showered on her, to grieve in her own way in her own time. What could be more understandable than that she should return to the country village where she'd spent so many childhood holidays?

Draining the fat from the eggs before adding them to the bacon and sausages already waiting on the heated plate beside her, she tossed a large slice of bread in the pan, pressing it down hard.

So she'd turned her back on her parents' elegant but unoccupied London apartment and arrived at Leamarsh, the print on her diploma hardly dry. Her original intention had been to stay at the cottage where she'd lived with Auntie Glover during the summer months when life had seemed so full of sunshine.

She smiled ruefully, turning the bread to expose its golden underside. The cottage had disappeared—a victim to development, replaced by a neat row of one-bedroomed starter houses.

It had been another bereavement. Stunned and unhappy, she'd traced her steps to the local inn, meaning to have a ploughman's lunch while she considered her next move, and it was there she'd learned about Amélie Benchard's stroke—and her need for a companion.

Of course she'd already known of Amélie's existence, seen her many times during her summer sojourns; listened to the friendly gossip about her foreign background, admired her style and charisma as she'd joined in the village activities, playing the role of lady of the Hall as if born into the British landed gentry. Hearing of her disability, Aphra had known instantly that she must go to her.

Theirs had been a healing relationship on both sides, she admitted silently. During those few brief months after Amélie had regained her full faculties they'd also shared the tragedies in their pasts, Amélie's wisdom and affection a much needed balm to the continuing ache in her own heart.

'Drat!' A drop of hot fat flew from the pan to settle on her hand, bringing her mind back sharply to the present as she turned the gas out, before using a spatula to add the fried bread to the appetising contents of the plate.

Salt, pepper, Worcester sauce... All were added to a tray already prepared with cutlery and a linen napkin, as she dwelt bitterly on how Amélie's worst nightmare had been realised.

Luc, either by design or misadventure, had forfeited his right to inherit, and his grandmother had been denied the opportunity to prevent the course of events she'd instigated, and latterly come to regret, from taking place.

Unless a miracle happened, Amélie's great-grandchildren would never play in the beautiful, scented garden she had created and tended with their future presence in mind. Unaccountably Aphra shivered.

Luc was reading the morning papers when she entered the conservatory to place the tray on the table in front of him.

'I thought you'd be more comfortable eating here than at the breakfast bar—and, as you know, the formal dining room's slightly overpowering for one person.'

'You won't join me, then?' His appreciative glance approved her offering before returning to rest questioningly on her face.

'No, thank you. I have to feed Sherlock and carry out various other duties which are expected of me by the trustees,' she said primly. 'It would be helpful if you could let me know what your plans are, so I can cater accordingly.'

She waited for his answer, standing stiffly, distancing herself emotionally from his disturbing presence.

'What would you suppose them to be, Aphra Grantly?' he queried, exasperation tingeing the deep timbre of his voice. Then as she hesitated, groping in her mind for something suitably noncommittal to suggest, he added, 'You've already judged me and found me wanting, kissed me and dismissed me. Surely you have some cynical thought about my future behaviour locked up in your quaint little mind? Now I'm inviting you to share it.'

'There's no need to be abusive!' She flinched beneath the sarcastic flick of his tongue. 'I don't work for you, and I don't have to answer your questions. For that matter, I don't have to let you in the house and I certainly don't have to feed you . . .'

'Debatable points.' The air between them seemed to hum with concentrated energy as he leant back in his chair. 'On the other hand, if your expressed feelings about who should be the new owner of this property are genuine, you won't want to see the back of me, will you? At least, not until the last possible day of my entitlement to claim the deeds has passed.'

'You've changed your mind?' Triumph and anguish seemed to collide in her solar plexus, causing her to catch her breath. 'You're going to ask some girl to marry you after all?'

'What a romantic you are, little Annie Glover.' There was no mercy in the tantalising smile he launched in her direction. 'No, I'm not. I am, however, presenting myself to the trustees to find out the full extent of my rights for the next fortnight preceding my thirty-first birthday, and to discover if they include the right to dispense with the no-longer required services of my grandmother's so-called companion!'

The temptation to pick up his breakfast, plate and all, and bring it down on top of his dark, arrogant head was almost impossible to resist. With an effort Aphra controlled her temper, but not before he'd read the desire for revenge in her outraged eyes.

'Try it and you'll collect more than a plate of fried eggs and bacon,' he warned her succinctly, the slight flick of his eyes marking a trail of scorn from the top of her head to the toes of her scuffed trainers.

For one dreadful moment, she felt herself quail beneath the contempt arrowed at her, then she saw the tenseness leave his body, the length of him relax.

Inwardly shaking, she drew in a deep breath in order to gain control of her voice. 'You'd be wasting your time,' she told him coldly. 'I'm quitting now.'

Turning abruptly, she made for the door. Her hand was already pulling it open when she heard his voice harsh and low behind her. 'I thought you might have guessed where I'd be going first thing this morning, Aphra. I'm going to the churchyard—to the family grave. I'm going to pay my last respects to Grand-mère.'

'Oh!' As she stood poised on the threshold words temporarily failed her, and she realised how deeply her apparent discounting of his pain had angered him.

She'd offered him no personal condolences, no opportunity to share his grief. He might have behaved thoughtlessly towards Amélie over the past months, but their closeness had been legendary in the village. She could scarcely blame Luc for

treating her with as little respect as she'd been prepared to give him.

'Yes, "oh",' he repeated sourly. 'And I said
nothing about ridding myself of your services—only
enquiring what my position would be if I desired
to do so. At the moment I don't. Until I've spoken
with Grand-mère's trustees I'd appreciate your remaining here until I have a clearer picture of the
situation.' His pause was infinitesimal. 'Don't
worry, I'll make it worth your while.'

'As you wish.' It was against all her instincts to
surrender to his request, but she owed him that, she
supposed, as part-payment for her insensitivity.
Besides, to walk out as she'd threatened would be
to break her agreement with the trustees. Never
mind that he was bound to consider her capitulation as being based on the promise of a reward!

She closed the door behind her, determined to
spend his absence devoting herself to the household
chores and banishing the image of his sardonic face
from her mind.

It wasn't as easy as she'd imagined, despite carrying her portable cassette player around the house
so that she could listen to her favourite light music
tapes as she dusted the beautiful walnut furniture,
made sure that the numerous mirrors sparkled and
that the high ceilings with the graceful ceiling drops
and architraves remained devoid of cobwebs.

To her surprise Luc had made his own bed. The
only sign of his occupation was the leather grip in
which he had presumably carried a change of
clothes. If he'd packed pyjamas, he must have

folded them neatly beneath his pillow. It wasn't an assumption she was about to check.

She left the bathroom to last, deciding to take a long, leisurely bath while she made up her mind as to whether she should make plans for providing him with lunch and dinner.

Amélie would certainly have expected nothing less of her, she admitted, opening the door and revealing that Luc's tidiness had extended to encompass that room too. Only a neatly boxed razor and tube of shaving soap beside a glass containing a toothbrush and tube of paste betrayed that he'd been there.

The towels she'd given him the previous evening had been neatly rehung and the bath itself had been rinsed and, from its shining appearance, dried out too. House-trained, then. At least she'd found one point in his favour! Repressing a small smile, she replaced the plug, turned the taps and began to disrobe.

By midnight, when she'd neither seen nor heard a word from the temporary heir to Fairmead Hall, that earlier momentary lessening of Aphra's antipathy towards him had well and truly disappeared. Where in heaven's name was he? she wondered as she decided to turn in for the night. Surely normal courtesy decreed that, having requested her to wait for his return, he could have let her know how late he'd be?

Justice forced her to admit that he hadn't requested her to prepare any meal for him. On the other hand, he might have guessed that she'd make suitable arrangements. Fortunately, the boeuf bourguignon she'd created wouldn't spoil. In fact its flavour would mature by tomorrow. That's if he should deign to put in another appearance at all. Perhaps in the face of her cool welcome, he'd found a more friendly environment in which to lay down his dark head!

It was Sherlock's deep growl from beyond her bedroom door which first alerted her to an alien presence outside. Struggling awake, she glanced at the luminous hands of her bedside clock. Two in the morning. A fine time to return! Or perhaps she had burglars? If so, then the burglar alarm she set every night would, hopefully, deter them. Grabbing her quilted silk dressing gown, she was searching for her slippers beneath the bed when the loud ringing of the doorbell dispelled her fears.

In moments she was on her way downstairs, disarming the alarm in the exclusion zone as she passed the control box.

'I got you out of bed.' Luc spared a moment to rake his eyes over her silk-clad figure and bare feet, before crossing the threshold. 'I'm sorry.'

Aphra shrugged. 'All-night discos haven't reached this corner of Kent yet,' she said, and was rewarded for her sarcasm by being subjected to a long, discerning appraisal, which left her feeling as if she'd been stripped, not only of her few clothes but of her mental privacy.

Suddenly self-conscious about the wealth of unbraided hair which drifted untidily around her shoulders, she began to back away from him. 'If there's nothing else you want tonight . . .'

'Oh, but there is, my dear Aphrodite. I want a large Scotch and your undivided attention.'

There was something about him, a kind of suppressed anger that was sending out high-level danger signals, which suggested she ignore the warning signs at her peril.

'Very well.' Tightening the belt which held her robe together, she decided to defuse the atmosphere, indicating he follow her to the conservatory. What were a glass of Scotch and a few minutes of her time, after all?

She switched on the low table-lamps, flooding the beautiful room with diffused light as Luc helped himself to the drink he required, tossing it down and refilling the glass before seating himself and reaching into the briefcase he'd abandoned on the floor, to produce a handful of newspapers. With a sharp movement of his wrist he flung them onto the table, indicating that she should examine them.

Puzzled, Aphra looked at the titles before confirming her opinion of their contents by flicking through the pages. 'They're full of classified advertisements.' Blankly she met the terrible bitterness reflected in his eyes. 'Am I supposed to look through them for another job?' It was a cruel way to confirm her dismissal, but she wouldn't let him see how deeply it hurt. She just hadn't imagined him to be that mean-spirited.

She winced as he let out an impatient breath and placed his glass on the table with unnecessary vigour. 'Don't be ridiculous, Aphra. I thought you'd realise what I intend to do, since you suggested it in the first place. After what I've discovered today, I accept there's no alternative open to me but to find a wife.'

Raising his whisky glass, he gesticulated towards the pile of newspapers he'd slung down. 'The newsagent assured me that those papers are full of invitations from nubile ladies seeking suitable mates. See what you can find for me.'

'It was an absurd idea...' Shocked, Aphra stared down at the stubborn set of his jaw. 'I should never have suggested it.' For some unknown reason her heart was pounding crazily. 'I just said the first thing that came into my head...' Her voice tailed off as she saw from his unmoving expression that he was paying no attention to her words.

'Luc, please...' She met his uncompromising eyes. 'I'm sure there are many genuine women who advertise in these columns, but how can you make your mind up about one in so little time?'

'I can't,' he returned harshly. 'But you can, Aphra, can't you? Dear God, but you saw through Marilyn within minutes of meeting her. You seem to have an instinct for detecting the genuine from the false. It's a skill I seem to be lacking.'

'I won't do it.' She closed her eyes for a fraction of a second, shutting out the bleak darkness of his obsidian gaze. 'I should never have said what I did. Yes, Amélie wanted you to inherit this place, but she'd never want you to tie yourself to a stranger— someone who could, by staying with you, make your life hell and, by divorcing you, could lay claim to half your fortune!'

She paused, her breath sawing in her throat, which seemed to have narrowed. Seeing nothing in

Luc's expression that indicated whether she was getting through to him, she persevered, anguish colouring her eager words.

'Of course she'd have hated to see Leonard living here, but that's not going to happen if he can't pay the inheritance tax, is it? I'm sure she'd rather strangers came and cared for the Hall than you put your life and future to hostage!'

'Possibly.' He stirred slightly. 'But, since you claim to have such intimate knowledge of her feelings, answer me this. How would Amélie have felt if she'd known that within months of her death Fairmead Hall would cease to exist; that it would be torn down, and its gardens excavated to make room for a development of up-market houses?'

'That's not possible!' Horror made Aphra's skin crawl as her voice strangled in her throat.

'More than possible. Almost a *fait accompli*. It wasn't easy, but I have good contacts in the right places. The facts are irrefutable. In anticipation of inheriting, Leonard has already come to an agreement with a developer. Plans have been drawn up and planning permission assured. Believe me, it's true. I've seen them.'

An ineffable madness replaced the bitterness in his tone. 'It's Leonard's final revenge on the woman he was raised to hate: destruction of everything she cared for, a rooting-out of what he was raised to see as an alien presence in his family tree.'

A slight, humourless smile touched his cruel mouth. 'But it isn't going to happen that way. However high the price of prevention, I won't allow it. So, tomorrow, little Annie Glover, I'd appre-

ciate your working through the "personal" advertisements and coming up with a short list.'

He rose suddenly, one stride eating the distance
between them, his hands reaching out to grasp her
shoulders. 'You do see the necessity, don't you?'
he demanded roughly. 'You claim to love this place
as much as Grand-mère did—as much as I do.
Now's your chance to prove it. Or do you want to
see the bulldozers moving in, tearing the trees out
by the roots, burying the shrubs which Amélie
planted with so much love?'

'No, no, of course I don't!' Her mind spinning,
her heart sick with the shock of what she'd just
been told, her reactions were too numbed to object
to his deprecatory use of the innocent alias she'd
used as a child.

Twisting around, she made an attempt to flee
from the brutal power of his fingers, unable to bear
the agony which distorted his dark, chiselled features, only to discover that it was impossible to
break free from his iron hold.

'So...' A muscle pulled spasmodically at his
jawline. 'I'll have to take my chance with the lonely
hearts ads, because there is only one other possible
solution which will preserve me from the unknown
horrors of sharing married intimacy with a total
stranger and at the same time enable me to claim
Fairmead Hall as my own.'

His tone altered, softened, as Aphra felt a sudden
tremor of a reckless, perverse excitement stream
through her.

He was too near, his warmth and his pain seeping
into her own body, unsteadying her, making it im-

possible to concentrate. Then, against all the most impossible odds, she heard him say, coolly, impersonally, 'And that is for *you* to become my obligatory bride.'

CHAPTER FOUR

SHOCK brought a warm tide of blood to Aphra's
face. A reaction not lost on her impertinent captor.

'All right—so as far as you're concerned I've just
crawled out from under a large stone,' Luc bit out.
'But look at it this way—at the moment you're redundant, with nowhere to live, and no means of
supporting yourself until you can find yourself
another position, and that's not going to be easy
in the present economic climate—especially without
a reference.'

Ignoring her sharp indrawn breath of outrage,
he continued smoothly, 'Marry me and you keep
the roof over your head, a guaranteed standard of
living for the immediate future and the promise of
a fair settlement in due course when the time comes
to end the charade.'

The sheer arrogance of his assumptions left her
speechless as she choked to find the words to disillusion him, to establish her financial
independence.

Nothing would please her more than to watch
the expression on his face as she told him about
the securities held in her name, the share portfolio
with which her parents had endowed her as a proof
of their responsibility for having brought her into
the world. As for his veiled threat to withhold a
reference...

'You—you...' she spluttered helplessly as she knew instinctively that he wouldn't believe a word of her protestations and that she had no immediate way of proving them true.

'Look, Aphra...' Impatiently he interrupted her. 'It's abundantly clear that you received no financial settlement from your first unfortunate venture into matrimony. You're too young and the marriage was too short to be of financial advantage to you.

'If you're expecting a legacy from my grandmother, then I have bad news for you. The solicitors tell me she left you nothing. Think about it! And if you're looking to Auntie Glover for help, I promise you my income outranks the state retirement pension.'

'Auntie Glover died three years ago.' Aphra stared at his arrogant countenance, appalled at his callousness.

'I'm sorry.' He had the grace to apologise, but the words were formal, offering her no comfort, serving only to stir her to further provocation.

'Of course there are always my parents,' she observed with forced brightness, managing to control the surging anger within her. 'I could throw myself on their mercy. I'm sure they wouldn't see me starve.'

'Parents?' He frowned. 'I never saw you with anyone else but Auntie Glover.' His tone was accusing. 'I thought you were an orphan.'

'Little orphan Annie?' The ridiculousness of the conversation dissipated her initial fury. Her mouth twitched with amusement. 'You do seem to have made rather a lot of suppositions about me in a very short time, Luc.'

'Not without some evidence, surely?' As if unwilling to admit he was at fault, he glared at her. 'If living at home was an option why didn't you go back when your marriage broke down?'

'Why do you think?' She shrugged off the relaxed pressure of his hands as she tilted her chin in confrontation, tempting him into voicing further evidence of his low opinion of her.

How could she tell him that her parents knew nothing about her brief and tragic sojourn into matrimony? What need had there been for her to mention the short, sad, simple service at Peter's bedside to them, when she'd known that within the week she would be widowed?

'They didn't approve of your marriage?' His eyes narrowed assessingly as he tried to translate the quizzical expression on her face. 'You quarrelled with them and either you're not welcome or you're too proud to admit they were right.'

She stared at him, unblinking. Even if she'd had the desire to throw herself into the bosom of her family, the Middle East was a long way to rush for the ostensibly affectionate but curiously emotionally distanced welcome she would have been likely to receive.

Wearily aware that she had gone too far to attempt an explanation anywhere near the truth, she gave a small, dismissive shrug. 'Something like that.'

'Then it makes sense for you to accept my offer.' His tone was terse, confident, as if he was masterminding a business deal—which, of course, he was, Aphra acknowledged, her eyes fixed on the bright intelligence of his expression as he made his case.

'You say you want to preserve the Hall, and, for what it's worth, I believe you're speaking the truth in that respect. Neither of us has any existing emotional commitment, so there's no conflict of interests there. Even after inheritance tax is paid, I shall be able to keep you in a style to which you would doubtlessly like to become accustomed, until such time as we can arrange a quiet divorce.' He paused slightly, then continued smoothly. 'Naturally, at the end of our arrangement, you would receive suitable compensation for your time and input.'

'Naturally.' Aphra's gaze lingered on the taut lines of his face as a slow, burning anger kindled deep inside her. He might have a share of the dark, animal magnetism which had attracted his grandfather to his young Corsican bride, but his arrogance was pure Benchard.

Quite apart from having the gall to suggest her complicity when he obviously detested the very sight of her, how dared he assume in such a high-handed manner that she had no existing emotional commitments? She might be no Kathryn Bellini, but that didn't mean that no man would look at her. Besides, looks weren't everything. For all he knew she could be having an affair with any one of the men in the village!

Suddenly, allied to her desperation to rescue Fairmead Hall from demolition, there was born, deep within her, the desire to tame that arrogance, to accept his incredible offer—and, when the time came, to spurn his largesse, to walk away empty-handed. It would be sweet revenge for his insults.

'For how long would this arrangement last?' Tilting her head slightly to one side, she watched the lines of tension ease from his forehead and knew he was sensing the odds against her acceptance of his bizarre suggestion shortening in his favour.

'Long enough to convince the lawyers that our marriage was genuine.' He shrugged. 'A year might be sufficient. Two years probably better. We can't afford to let Leonard scent a conspiracy or he'll move heaven and earth to accuse us of collusion to cheat him of his just inheritance. Believe me, he'd make a bitter and persistent enemy.'

His smile was cruel, without humour. 'Play the game according to the rules and your reward will be great. Give Leonard cause to doubt your sincerity and there could be hell to pay—for both of us.' His dark, intelligent eyes dwelt questioningly on her pale face.

'I could always refuse to play at all.' She returned his gaze, hoping against hope to discern some compassion or understanding in its depths, but there was only a muted glimmer of triumph, as if he already knew that his cause was won.

'No, *ma chère*, not you.' There was nothing affectionate in the endearment as he shook his dark head slowly from side to side. 'I think I know you better than that. If the stakes are high enough, you'll play. And in this case we both know how high they are.' There was an infinitesimal pause before he spoke again, as if he was waiting for his words to sink in and register on her avarice. 'So, Aphra—do we shake on it?'

He held out an imperious hand.

For an instant she closed her eyes, unsettled by the rapid pounding of her heart. How could anyone in her right mind accept such a damning proposition? Then, as if in a dream, she heard her own voice, low and controlled.

'For Amélie's sake,' she said coolly, and touched her palm against Luc's.

'Who else's?' The sarcastic query was not meant to be answered as he pulled her abruptly against his own body, cupping her chin with his free hand so that she was in no position to resist the touch of his mouth against her own.

She opened her lips to protest, but no words came as he sealed their bargain with a deeply searching kiss. Breathless and shaken, she staggered slightly as he released her. Conscious that the belt confining her robe had slipped and the edges parted, she fumbled with trembling hands to cover the revealing silk of her nightdress.

She should have felt violated by his insolent actions; instead she felt only confused. A tremor of shame trembled through her veins as she realised how near to total humiliation she'd come. Another second and she would have returned his kiss instead of meekly accepting it.

'I—you . . .' she began weakly, feeling she should voice some kind of protest at his action but unable to find the words which would help her to regain her dignity.

'Go to bed, Aphra.' It was a command. A presage of what she could expect in the coming days? 'It's been a long day. We'll discuss arrangements tomorrow.'

The cinnamon-coloured silk suit looked fabulous, as indeed it should, considering how much she'd spent on it. Just one week later, Aphra observed her reflection in the old-fashioned pier-glass in her bedroom at Fairmead. The slimline skirt, fully lined, of course, ended flatteringly just below her kneecaps, whilst the loose jacket with its exquisitely stitched collar and revers and three-quarter-length cuffed sleeves was casual enough to be comfortable without appearing too informal for such an important occasion.

Luc had instructed her to spare no expense when buying a suitable outfit for the marriage ceremony, and she'd obeyed him, accepting the supposed privilege of becoming a second signatory to his gold card without batting an eyelid.

At least his assumption that she was divorced had prevented him from considering a wedding at the local church. Or perhaps, like herself, Luc had reservations about the degree of hypocrisy in which he was prepared to indulge!

She sighed. Fortunately, for her peace of mind, her 'fiancé' had left Fairmead for London the day after she'd accepted his startling proposal and she hadn't set eyes on him since.

Not that she hadn't spoken to him. Her mouth twisted in a wry smile as she recalled the twice-daily phone calls he'd made to her during his absence, ostensibly to check that she'd been following his myriad instructions for the great day, dictated at some length before his departure, but in truth, she suspected, to ensure that she hadn't changed her mind.

She smiled wryly again. Would Luc recognise her when she stepped out of the white Rolls-Royce? Even she'd gasped in astonishment when the recently departed hairdresser had allowed her to look in the mirror. Because of the fineness of her hair it hadn't been necessary to cut it to achieve the bouncing tumble of blonde waves which swirled around her shoulders and nudged her professionally made-up face. Amazing what a few deft touches from experts could achieve!

Moving carefully on the spindly three-inch-high heels of her hand-tooled Florentine leather shoes, she made her way to the dressing table, easing herself down on the satin-covered stool to survey her complexion with critical eyes.

Subtle yet effective, she decided—as one would expect from an expert from such a well-known cosmetic company.

The light, creamy foundation had been applied with a damp sponge, so thinly that it merely enhanced her unblemished skin, but it was the delicate dusting of grey eye-shadow and two coats of mascara which had really revolutionised her appearance, turning an unexceptional English rose into a more exotic bloom.

Experimentally she smiled at her image, peeping at her reflection from demurely lowered lashes, seeing unexpected dimples appear in her cheeks as she strove to hold back her laughter at the effects achieved by artifice.

Thinking of roses, she hoped Luc would approve of her perfume—a light, delicate fragrance which she'd used sparingly, not because it was expensive, which it was, but because, as she'd already told him, she didn't care for heavy fragrances.

Eleven-thirty. She suppressed a shiver. Soon the car would be arriving to take her to her bridegroom. A spasm of fear lanced through her. She must be mad! What other reason could there be for her marrying a stranger for the sole purpose of preserving a pile of bricks and mortar?

But Luc wasn't a stranger. She'd heard so much about him, witnessed some of his triumphs and disasters, seen him cope with victory and adversity with a careless grace and good humour which had endeared him to her. But oh, so long ago... Now he was older, embittered, still in love with Kathryn Bellini...

She moved uneasily as waves of doubt began to flow through her veins. Breathing in deeply in an attempt to quieten the rising panic that threatened to swamp her, she forced herself to think of other things, recalling the way in which her parents had reacted when she'd telephoned them with her news.

'That's marvellous, darling!' her mother had exclaimed. 'Frankly I always hoped you'd see sense and make a good marriage. What kind of career is speech therapy for a woman anyway?'

'I wish you both every happiness, Aphra.' Her father's deep voice could have been that of a stranger for all the emotion it carried. 'Naturally your mother and I won't be able to make the ceremony at such short notice—but we'll be thinking of you.'

At least they weren't offended by her abrupt decision—but then she hadn't expected them to be. As for thinking of her—of course they would, and later there would be an expensive gift ordered and delivered from Harrods. That was the way it had always been.

She started as the front doorbell echoed through the house. The car, perhaps? Someone would find out and tell her. After all, the Hall was a mass of activity as caterers and florists added the last-minute touches to their preparations. If they found it strange that she should be sitting upstairs all alone on the morning of her wedding day then it was not their business to remark on it.

Although she had no close relations many of her friends from school and college would be at the register office awaiting her arrival. Besides, she'd never feel alone in this house because it was imbued with Amélie's love and passion for life.

'Ms Grantly?' A light knock at the door interrupted her thoughts.

'Come in.' She sprang to her feet as the door opened to reveal a pretty brunette dressed in an immaculate waitress's uniform.

'A messenger just delivered these, Ms Grantly. He said you should open them immediately.'

Taking the two small, plain-wrapped packages, Aphra thanked her, waiting until she'd left the room before opening the larger of the two to reveal an ivory-throated orchid, its reflex petals blotched with subtle shades of cinnamon. The card accompanying it bore Luc's distinctive signature.

Pleasure warmed her before she realised it was all part of the act, the charade they were mounting to preserve his heritage. With a small grimace of resignation, she laid it aside and began to unwrap the smaller parcel.

Inside an outer box were two smaller ones, one a long oval, the other a leather-covered ring box, the edges scuffed, the fine gold imprint on the lid worn with time.

Curious, Aphra opened the oval box first, and caught her breath. Inside was a single strand of gradated pearls, their deep lustre and fine gradation betraying their value. Reverently she replaced them in their satin bed before opening the remaining box to discover, inside a nest of black satin, a gold ring set with a solitaire yellow diamond. It was only then that she saw the folded sheet of paper which had accompanied the packages.

'Something old, something new...' Luc had written. 'These are old. Both belonged to Amélie and my grandfather's mother before her. They have been kept in the bank pending a new mistress at Fairmead. Please wear them this morning at the ceremony. Leonard will expect it.'

That was all. He had sent her the trappings of love without one word of encouragement for the ordeal ahead, but what had she expected? As far as he was concerned, she was being paid well for her services. There was no requirement that he had to be civil to her as well!

She was staring contemplatively from the window, when she saw the beribboned bonnet of the Rolls emerge from the cluster of shrubs which guarded the wrought-iron gates of the drive. Inhaling a deep breath, she took one last look around the room in which she'd spent so many contented hours during her short time as Amélie's friend and companion.

The next time she entered it, it would be as mistress of Fairmead Hall.

Fifteen minutes later she was stepping from the Rolls-Royce, composed and elegant, only to pause in astonishment as she realised that the crowd of people—gathered at the entrance to the old Georgian mansion which had been reclaimed and renovated by the local authorities for use as a register office—was awaiting her arrival.

She had expected only twenty or so intimate friends and business acquaintances of Luc together with a handful of her own friends to attend the ceremony, although invitations to the reception at Fairmead Hall had been extended to the entire village.

Now it seemed that they'd all turned out to see the bride arrive.

For a brief second, images of her earlier wedding flashed across Aphra's mind—the gaily decorated hospital ward a stark contrast to the pallor of Peter's face, her pretty cotton dress mocking a service which had hallowed a union without a future. Now, for the second time in her life she was taking part in a charade.

Only vaguely aware of the spatter of background applause which greeted her descent from the car, she hesitated at the entrance to the glass-roofed, flower-bedecked arcade which she knew led towards the antechamber of the marriage room.

Suppose Luc hadn't arrived? Suppose he'd changed his mind? Was this hope or fear? She was uncertain as her heart lurched alarmingly at the prospect of a public humiliation, and then she saw him, walking towards her, his long, leonine strides eating the distance between them until he was close enough to take her free hand—the one which wasn't clutching the tiny handbag which was more accessory than necessity—and entwine his strong fingers through her own.

'You got the orchid—good.' His voice was low, caressing, a burr of pleasure for the benefit of the people close enough to catch its timbre, but his eyes were hard and calculating.

'How clever of you to get the colour right, Luc,' she simpered up at him, aware of how his fingers had tautened against her own.

'Not really.' He dismissed her compliment with lazy disregard. 'An orchid is one of those rare accessories which is so perfect that it can never clash with anything else that is worn.' There was a barely perceptible pause before he added, 'As well as being one of nature's more erotic blooms.'

'Surely you mean exotic?' she queried sweetly, aware that, with an expression of melting sweetness, his dark eyes were taking a careful note of her expensive make-up and hairdo, but uncertain whether he approved or not. Not that it was of any real concern to her because she was confident enough of her own taste not to be embarrassed by his disapproval anyway.

'Do I?' His thumb had centred on her palm and was rubbing it gently. 'I don't think so, but it's something we can discuss at a more appropriate time. Thank you for wearing the Benchard pearls and diamond.'

'My pleasure.' She shrugged, relieving the build-up of tension which had held them rigid. 'Like you said, expensive items can never be vulgar.'

'Wrong, my love.' Something flared behind his bland expression but his beautiful mouth retained its smile; only the hard pressure of his fingers tightening against her hand, crushing the diamond ring between them, suggested he was irritated by her comment. 'If you're going to paraphrase me, you must do it correctly.'

'Then you'll have to teach me how,' she returned sweetly, masking the sudden spurt of anger she felt tightening her diaphragm. Did he really believe that she cared one iota for the value of the jewellery he had allowed her to wear? With a quick movement of her arm, she withdrew her hand from his clasp, raising it to touch the perfect pearls encircling her neck. They were Amélie's pearls; that was what mattered. Everything she was doing today was for Amélie.

Luc's low laugh was short, honeyed with amusement. 'Believe me, Aphra, in the next few months I'm going to take a great deal of pleasure in teaching you a good many things.'

It sounded like a threat and the sharp glint lurking at the back of his sable eyes did nothing to quieten her sudden misgivings. For one wild moment she wanted to turn and run, cleave her way through the small crowd of people in their bright, summery clothes, run until she was back in the sanctuary of the rose garden at Fairmead... She must have been mad to believe for one moment that she could bring this imperious stranger to heel.

'Too late. Too late for regrets, Aphra.' Swiftly Luc seized her arm, his voice scarcely more than a whisper yet penetrating to her very soul. 'The only way you step foot over the threshold of Fairmead again is as my wife.'

'You don't think I want to change my mind, do you? Not after all the hard work I've put into making the arrangements?' She tilted her head, smiling up at him, hoping he would see the lifted corners of her lips rather than the blankness behind her eyes. 'Aphra Benchard, mistress of Fairmead Hall—it has quite a ring to it, doesn't it?'

'Almost as exciting as Aphra Benchard, mistress of Luc Benchard,' he agreed, swiftly parrying her thrust with a sword which pricked at her heart.

'That wasn't part of the agreement and you know it!' Her mouth suddenly dry, she dropped her bantering tone. 'Why are we standing here talking, Luc? Isn't the registrar ready for us yet?'

'Relax, darling.' To her sensitive ears the endearment sounded scathing. 'How many weddings do you think take place at a small-town register office in mid-week? We're the only act on the bill today.'

'Then why—?'

'Photographers, Aphra. People like to take photographs of the bride arriving as well as departing.'

'Oh!' For the first time she became aware of cameras in the crowd of well-wishers, but, more than that, whilst she and Luc had been conducting their soft conversation, three obviously professional photographers had emerged into the space surrounding them and were happily snapping away.

'Where did they come from?' she asked, amazed. 'I didn't hire photographers!'

'Your first mistake,' Luc returned equably. 'Who ever heard of a wedding without a photographer? It's a good job I anticipated your reluctance to put the event on film and made my own arrangements, as well as notifying the local press. Now give me a bright, loving smile and look as if you're pleased to see me, before the onlookers think we're having a row.'

But wasn't that exactly what they were doing? She bared her teeth at him in the mockery of a smile.

'Cousin Leonard's here.' Luc's voice, low and urgent, pierced her thoughts as, taking her hand, he led her towards the entrance. 'So make it look good, sweetheart. Remember your future prosperity depends on how good an actress you are!'

The ceremony was short, over almost before she'd realised it had begun. A civil agreement before witnesses. Thankfully with no implied requirement to love or to honour, no pledges about sickness or health, no empty words about richer or poorer...

In a daze Aphra repeated the short phrases necessary to make her the legal wife of Luc Benchard, feeling only a dreadful emptiness as she signed the register and stepped back to allow the two witnesses to append their signatures.

'I believe tradition decrees I kiss my new bride, hmm?' Unlike during their previous conversation, Luc's voice was deliberately loud, commanding the attention of the guests as he slid his arm around her waist, his hand finding its way beneath her jacket to rest on the delicate Indian voile of the inexpensive blouse she'd chosen in a small high-street boutique for no better reason than that she'd fallen in love with its soft blur of tans, blues and green.

Obediently she raised her face towards him, knowing it was expected, part of the act to avoid the accusation of collusion. She was anticipating a cursory touching of lips, so that when one of Luc's hands moved up to her face to capture her chin and compel her startled gaze to meet him she stared back helplessly into the black void of his eyes.

She was so close to him, so aware of the sheer maleness which emanated from him that her breath caught in her throat in dismay, every nerve in her system responding to the length of his body as it encroached on her own space.

'Luc...' Half protesting, half pleading, she parted her lips as all her senses signalled panic. Then his mouth descended, accepting an offer she'd never meant to extend, as both his powerful hands lowered to caress her form through the thin material which covered it, moulding her brazenly against him, proclaiming his domination to every amused spectator in the room.

For a brief moment there was nothing in her universe but the heat of Luc's body, the mastery of his hands, the ardent possession of his mouth as he aroused then satisfied her sudden aching hunger which surged to meet and match his ardour. Then she was remembering where she was, realising that Luc was making a deliberate and cold-blooded exhibition of her before their friends—and, worse still, that her ability to prevent him was limited.

Her body went rigid, but it seemed there was no way she could escape the vice-like grip in which he held her, whilst his lips continued their savage exploration of her mouth in what, it appeared to her heightened sensibilities, was rapidly becoming a public humiliation.

Just when she thought her only escape would be to feign a blackout, Luc suddenly released her. Somewhere behind her she heard indulgent laughter, a whisper of understanding, friendly applause, but she had eyes only for Luc's face. His eyes were narrowed, without sparkle—empty voids concealing both thought and motive. But his lips, those sweet, heartbreaking curves of warm flesh, were twisted contemptuously.

As a deep, inexplicable fear stirred in her heart, Aphra staggered on her high heels. Immediately Luc supplied support, dipping his dark head towards her, the very image of a caring and devoted new husband.

Over his shoulder, she could see a middle-aged man standing alone by the door, and guessed from his age, appearance and dour attitude that he must be Leonard. So that was why Luc had acted out his little floor show. It had been a pointed and public demonstration of a private victory, exhibiting a bitter ruthlessness which nothing she'd previously known about him had led her to expect.

In her innocence she'd believed she'd agreed to wed an acquaintance from the past, a man whose ethics were close to her own. She was wrong. She had married a total stranger. And a dangerous one at that.

CHAPTER FIVE

'YOU might have let me into the secret earlier!' Two hours into the reception Liz Matthews scolded Aphra in mock disapproval, a glass of champagne in one hand, a smoked salmon titbit in the other. 'All those years we spent together playing lacrosse as children and you never let slip one word about the lord of the manor!'

Standing close to the exotic orange-flowering hibiscus which had been one of Amélie's favourite plants amongst the varied contents of the conservatory, Aphra laughed at her friend's outraged expression. 'Oh, that's because I was waiting to grow up and catch his attention myself,' she lied, drinking deeply from her own champagne glass, silently congratulating herself on her choice of wine.

As one of her few confidantes Liz had been made privy to the reasons for her doomed marriage to Peter. She had understood the pain and grief involved, had been quietly supportive when the inevitable had happened. Now she was bubbling over with more effervescence than the wine in her glass.

'Very understandable.' Liz nodded enthusiastically. 'If I'd had something as potentially beautiful growing in my own backyard I wouldn't have allowed trespassers either! Talk about a whirlwind romance, though. The last time I spoke to you on the phone you were acting as companion to his grandmother, and when I asked you if she had any relatives you told me that she had a grandson who was too busy enjoying himself on a world tour to even send her a card.'

'Yes, well...' Embarrassed at the repetition of her own words, Aphra sought to remove the sting of her condemnation. 'That turned out to be a hasty judgement,' she excused herself glibly. 'I wasn't in full possession of the facts.'

'Which were?' Liz's brown eyes sparkled with inquisitiveness.

'Confidential.' Aphra's quick rebuff was accompanied by a flashing smile which took any offence from it. Already she was learning her role, and, truth to tell, enjoying playing the part. It was a challenge to her natural creativity, she realised with surprise—another opportunity for her emotional need to nurture and preserve.

'But obviously totally altruistic.' Liz accepted the reproach with the true charity of a close friend, changing tack with barely a pause. 'Who on earth are all these people?'

'Mainly the inhabitants of Leamarsh,' Aphra confessed with a wry twist of her mouth.

'Having the time of their lives!' Liz said approvingly. 'Although I have to say that the gentleman standing over there by the window appears to be the exception. He looks more like the spectre at the feast. Do you think I should go over and try to cheer him up?'

'No, no, I don't think that would be a good idea!' Aphra's quick glance had identified a granite-faced

Leonard. 'As a matter of fact he's Luc's cousin—well, his father's cousin really.'

Liz's raised eyebrows invited her to supply an explanation.

'I'm afraid he doesn't approve of the marriage.' Anxious not to be questioned further on the matter, she hurried on, 'You've already been introduced to Mike, one of the witnesses, haven't you? He's an old friend of Luc's—'

'Mmm, and his wife and two little daughters,' Liz agreed philosophically. 'More's the pity. Doesn't your delicious groom have any unmarried friends?'

'Not that I know of—not close ones anyway.'

'What about the disagreeable father's cousin? No dark and dashing heir there?'

''Fraid not.' Aphra shook her head, liking the unusual feel of her soft hair brushing against her cheek. Pity that after a night pressed into a pillow it would revert to its usual soft fly-away state. 'Leonard and Barbara have never had children.' An errant thought strayed into her mind. Suppose Leonard had been a father? Would he have wanted to hand down Fairmead to his own child, or would he still have chosen to destroy it and with it every trace of Amélie—the usurper?

She'd always imagined that Luc had inherited his tenacity from the Corsican blood in his veins. Now for the first time, she wondered whether the cruel streak so evident in the other branch of the Benchards was, like the arrogance she had detected, also part of his genetic make-up. It was a thought which added to her apprehension for the future.

'Well, don't look so depressed about it,' Liz responded lightly. 'I'm not that desperate to marry into money. After all, we're all emancipated now, aren't we? In theory I can make my own pile and enjoy it without having to pander to a man's baser instincts.'

'Is that what people are going to believe I did?' Aphra's fingers tightened around the stem of her glass.

'You?' Liz's eyes widened in astonishment. 'Why on earth should they believe that? Quite apart from the fact that your family are rolling in it, it's quite obvious to everyone that you and Luc are magically in love. That kiss after the ceremony? Phew! A score of nine point nine on the Richter scale.'

A warmth not entirely due to the amount of champagne she had sipped flooded into Aphra's cheeks. 'I apologise for that,' she said stiffly. 'It was in very bad taste.'

'Rubbish!' Liz dismissed her words with scant regard. 'It was very refreshing. An impulsive, uncontrollable manifestation of lust within the social bounds of marriage. Who could possibly object to that?'

'Someone who spent their formative years in a convent school for girls?'

'Nonsense!' The other girl grinned. 'That kind of education gives one a very special insight into sensual behaviour. Forbidden fruit and all that.'

'You're incorrigible.' Aphra's smile gave the lie to her reproof, as inwardly she acknowledged the truth behind Liz's words. Delay the pleasure and its enjoyment becomes greater... It had been one of the maxims passed on to her by Auntie Glover and one which she'd readily adopted into her life. If nothing else, it had prevented her from rushing headlong into situations which might later bring her regret. Until now, of course...

'No. Just jealous,' the other girl vouchsafed cheerfully. 'Your parents couldn't make it, then?'

'You know how it is.' Aphra shrugged, fully aware that Liz, who was a member of a close family group, hadn't the slightest idea what it was like to float around in an emotional vacuum. It was warm and well ordered, but a vacuum nevertheless. 'My father's deeply involved in a mining project survey in the middle of nowhere. He can't just pack up and leave at a moment's notice.'

'And you couldn't delay the wedding long enough for him to make other arrangements, hmm?'

'Luc doesn't believe in long engagements.' Aphra made a small *moue* of resignation, glad that the terms of Amélie's will weren't common knowledge.

'Nor in staying too long at one's own reception!' She heard his voice at the same time as his arm slid across her shoulders. 'I think it's about time we thought of leaving, sweetheart.' A swift impression on her nervous system of his nearness, the scent of his skin and hair against her cheek, then the swift, sharp shock of feeling his immaculate teeth gently nip at her earlobe brought a small cry of protest to Aphra's lips.

'For heaven's sake, *darling*.' She used the endearment with heavy irony as Liz's eyes glowed with amusement at the intimate caress. 'Do you have to be so physical in public?'

'Of course.' His eyebrows raised in mock surprise. 'Marriage is a very physical state of existence. I don't think our guests are going to be shocked just because I nuzzle my wife's ear, do you? They'd probably be more shocked if I didn't.' He included Liz in the bright seductiveness of his smile. 'By the same token they'll understand my haste to spirit you away to a romantic rendezvous where I can be even more physical in private without offending your delicate susceptibilities.'

'Away where?' Aphra met his normally expressive eyes suspiciously. Confronted by their blandness, she felt prickles of alarm escalate up and down her spine. Nothing had been said about leaving Fairmead and she'd simply assumed they'd keep their own rooms and continue living much as before.

'That depends.' He regarded her musingly. 'Do you have a current passport?'

Fixed by his sparkling, interrogative gaze, she was unhappily aware of Liz's inquisitive appraisal of her response—aware, too, that Liz knew perfectly well that, since she'd been in the habit of spending Christmas holidays with her parents in the past, it was unlikely she would have let such an important document lapse.

'Yes.' It was the only answer she could give without leaving herself open to surprised comment from her best friend. If Luc preferred to believe that her motives in marrying him were partially activated by greed, then she was in no mood to let him discover otherwise—especially via an intermediary!

'Excellent!' He nodded his approval. 'In that case, the answer to your question is—wherever our fancy takes us.'

'A secret honeymoon—how romantic and exciting!' Liz's eyes sparkled mischievously as she made no attempt to hide her admiration of Luc either as a man or as a bridegroom. 'In your own private Lear jet, of course?'

He shook his head, allowing his own gaze to move appreciatively over Liz's trim figure as his lips twisted into a wolfish smile. 'Unfortunately, since my company was floated on the Stock Exchange, the shareholders own fifty per cent of that. I'm afraid Aphra and I are going to have to make other arrangements.'

'First class, I hope.' The querulousness in Aphra's voice was not assumed, although the reason for it had nothing to do with the mode of travel she could expect. How could Liz flirt so outrageously with Luc, and, worse still, how dared Luc so obviously enjoy her posturing? On Liz's part it was pure fun—she didn't doubt that for one moment—but for Luc to respond with such overt charm was a little too much to bear.

'What else, darling?' There was an expression behind the dark, velvety eyes as they turned to appraise her which she couldn't readily translate. 'But don't worry—you're not going to be trapped inside a metal carcase for twenty-four hours.'

'Not Australia, then?' She mounted a pout of assumed disappointment. 'I've always wanted to explore the Great Barrier Reef.'

'A worthy ambition, Aphra.' Luc's dark head nodded approvingly. 'But one which will have to wait a little longer to be fulfilled. On this occasion we'll be exploring territory much closer to hand.'

'I'd settle for that.' Again Liz intervened, her laughing eyes making a knowing appraisal of Luc's superb body, its physical perfection only masked by the elegant suit which clothed it.

Ashamed by the wave of irritation which rose to disturb her equanimity, Aphra found it impossible to curb the sharpness of her tongue. 'In that case, I suggest *you* go away with Luc,' she told her friend with a marked degree of asperity. 'I'm perfectly content to stay here at Fairmead and do some gardening.'

'Ooh! That sounds like fighting talk!' Liz's pretty face was alight with amused interest. Clearly she believed she was witnessing the kind of verbal foreplay which would eventually lead to a passionate and loving physical showdown. For the first time in their long friendship Aphra experienced a decided irritation towards the other girl.

'Not really,' Luc intervened, his deep voice low and soft, loaded with false consideration. 'Naturally Aphra's concerned about what will happen to the garden in her absence. It holds a very special place in her heart—especially since it was the scene of our reunion after a long separation.' His tender mouth found her cheek in a soft salutation which made her grit her teeth. 'Relax, sweetheart, everything's being taken care of—from cancelling the milk to finding a good temporary home for Sherlock. Your beloved garden will continue to be well tended.' His lips left her face as his arm dropped to imprison her waist, holding her firmly against him.

'Now, if you'll excuse us, Liz, we've got some packing to do, before we slip away and leave the party. Mike's accepted the role of Master of Ceremonies and I can assure you there's a lot more fun to come, so I hope you can stay to the end.' His tone was warm and welcoming. 'There'll be more people coming later on, when they get back from work, and I've arranged for a couple of local groups to provide live music for dancing. Hopefully, there'll be something for everybody's taste.'

'But you'll come back and say goodbye officially before leaving?' Liz's face was a picture of dismay. 'I mean, you're not just going to steal away like two thieves in the night?'

'Of course not,' Luc reassured her. 'We'll let you wave us farewell, but if you're thinking of decorating our going-away car, forget it. It's not even within shouting distance.'

So everything was under control, was it? Aphra's body was rigid with anger as she allowed Luc to guide her through the chattering throng. Only when they'd safely negotiated the crowd downstairs and had reached the upper landing did she turn to confront him, her eyes flashing with ill-concealed annoyance.

'I don't know what you're playing at, Luc,' she began heatedly, feeling a warm pulse of anger beating at her throat.

' "For better for worse"?' he suggested silkily, his grip on her upper arm firming as he guided her the last few steps towards her bedroom door, opening it with his free hand and propelling her across the threshold. 'I can give you one hour to pack.'

An aching fury catching at her throat as she met his implacable gaze, Aphra tilted her head back in steely confrontation. 'If this is the ''worse'', then I don't think a lot of it!'

'It's the ''better'', Aphra,' he returned softly. 'And you'd *better* get used to it unless it's your ambition to see a cul-de-sac of contemporary houses replacing Fairmead.'

'I don't need reminding of that fact.' She wrenched her arm from his grasp, moving further into the room, a shiver of regret trembling through every cell of her body as she glimpsed the abandoned orchid container. Empty and meaningless— like the substance of her marriage. 'I told you I'd co-operate and I will, but I expect some consideration and respect in return.'

'As well as a rise in your standard of living?' His dark eyebrows rose mockingly. 'You drive a hard bargain, my Aphrodite, but, rest assured, you shall have everything that it is in my power to give you.'

The words were smoothly delivered, but the message behind them was there for anyone with intuition to read and translate, the sterility of emotion staring her in the face. Not only was Luc still in love with Kathryn Bellini, but the injury the other woman had delivered to his heart was still raw, and on top of that grief he was still suffering the remorse of losing Amélie. Luc was telling her he could give her nothing, not even the courtesy of considering her feelings.

'A little more notice of your intentions and time to prepare for them would have been a courteous gesture.' A nervous little pulse was beating in her throat as she met his unrepentant gaze. 'It's very inconsiderate of you to spring your plans on me like that, in front of a witness. Didn't it occur to you that I might prefer to stay here?'

'Of course it did,' he agreed amiably. 'Which is why I didn't trouble to seek your opinion.' His supercilious regard made her hackles rise. 'In theory marriage is an equal partnership. In practice one partner usually takes the initiative; it's the natural order of life. I just wanted to make sure you realised that on this occasion my decision wasn't open to discussion.'

'Why?' Aphra tilted her chin at him. 'Isn't it enough that legally you've satisfied the terms of Amélie's will, without our having to go through the farce of a mock honeymoon?'

'Use your intelligence, Aphra!' he said impatiently. 'You saw Leonard's face at the ceremony. You must have felt the anger, frustration and hate emanating from him at the reception. For pity's sake—he'd just seen a fortune disappearing from his grasp! Do you really believe that he's going to accept the situation if there's the slightest chance he can do something about it?'

'Like claiming conspiracy to defraud, you mean?' she asked doubtfully. 'But... I don't see how our staying here would have given him grounds—'

'No?' Sarcasm sharpened the monosyllable. 'In separate rooms? With you continuing in your role of cook-housekeeper, not to mention chief gardener? Is that what you thought was going to happen? How convincing would that have appeared to the friendly and inquisitive natives of Leamarsh?'

'They wouldn't have known,' she said painfully, deliberately refraining from reminding him that her role had been that of companion, that Amélie had also employed a home help and a gardener. Any labours she had carried out within the house had been inspired by love, not duty. 'About the separate rooms, I mean. As for the rest—aren't those functions that many wives willingly carry out?'

'Not mine,' he retorted grimly. 'And you're even more naïve than I suspected if you truly believe that we wouldn't have become the victims of damaging gossip if, after marrying my grandmother's employee, I'd continued to employ her in a domestic role immediately after our nuptials.'

Unwilling to acknowledge his logic although she was beginning to see his point, she began argumentatively, 'Other people—'

'And that's another reason,' he interrupted her tersely, a spark of antagonism flaring in the depths of his eyes. 'We need time together, away from distractions, to work out a plan for civilised coexistence. My tolerance won't extend to allowing you to question every decision I make or to scold me as if I were some recalcitrant child.'

The bleak reminder of the way she'd greeted him on his return to the Hall sent a pinprick of remorse to her heart. Perhaps if she'd known then of his estrangement from La Bella Bellini she would have been more tolerant.

On the other hand, since he saw himself as such a dominant figure, he ought to have found an inner strength to consider someone else apart from himself, oughtn't he?

Unwilling to concede moral defeat, she managed to conjure up an amused smile.

'Do I do that, Luc?' She widened her eyes in mock surprise. 'If so, it's probably because during my original training as a speech therapist I specialised in the treatment of children. Sometimes it's necessary to be firm with them when they're uncooperative or deliberately obtuse. It's a habit that's difficult to break, I'm afraid.'

She sighed, lowering her lashes to hide the sparkle of irritation she was sure would be evident. Children weren't the only problem either, she recalled sadly, recollecting Amélie's frustrated inability to make herself understood in the early days after her first stroke, and her consequent bad temper.

'Exactly!' he exclaimed triumphantly. 'Which is why we're going somewhere quiet and unobserved while you come to terms with that problem. And, believe me, darling, I don't intend to leave you under any illusion as to my status as a fully grown, adult man.' Luc's quick retort, though softly spoken, was nothing if not a threat. 'By the time we return I'm sure you'll be an expert in convincing all our acquaintances, friendly or otherwise, that ours is truly a love match.'

Nervously Aphra took a step away from him. Whatever she'd expected from him, it hadn't been this aggressive, almost punitive attitude. Clearly his mind was made up and there was no profit in continuing her argument. Aware of the tight rein on which he appeared to be keeping his temper, discretion was most certainly the better part of valour.

'So—where exactly are we going?' she asked coolly. 'What kind of things am I expected to take with me at a moment's notice?'

Luc shrugged. 'I thought you might have guessed. The occasion seemed an appropriate one to introduce my wife to the other roots from which I sprang.'

'Corsica?' He could hardly mean anywhere else, she surmised as a thrill of excitement warmed her blood, momentarily overcoming her irritation at his high-handedness. 'Oh, Luc, that's wonderful! Amélie told me so much about it...'

'I'm glad you approve.' The glint of amusement in his eyes taunted her with the knowledge that her approval hadn't been necessary to his plans. 'However, I think I should warn you that we won't be staying at a first-class hotel in one of the glamorous resorts. My grandmother was born in a small mountain village east of the Gulf of Porto—not unknown to tourists now, but still a far cry from the yachts and ostentatious wealth of the larger coastal resorts. So you needn't make plans to augment your wardrobe. A pair of jeans, a couple of cotton tops, a warm sweater in case of unfriendly winds and a pair of tough-soled walking shoes should suffice.'

His gaze drifted downwards to regard her slender feet encased in the high-heeled leather, before returning to her face with a deprecatory smile. 'You'll find the village roads are steep and stony, and some of the natural vegetation a trifle thorny.'

'We're going on a hiking tour, then?' she enquired brightly, spurred on by his patronising attitude. 'If you'd warned me a little earlier I would have bought myself a rucksack. Or do you recommend I pack my meagre wardrobe in a plastic carrier from the local supermarket?'

'A small suitcase will do fine.' He ignored her sarcasm as if it was beneath his dignity to react to it—which, she determined miserably, it probably was. 'Laundry won't be a problem for you; most things dry quickly in the wind and the sun. The only other items I'd recommend as necessities would be a toothbrush and a change of underwear.'

'It sounds a delightful spot for a honeymoon.' Aphra offered him a bright, meaningless smile. 'I can't wait to see it. What a good job I've got a passport.'

'Yes, isn't it?' he agreed smoothly. 'Though your lack of one would only have delayed my plans for another twenty-four hours. It would hardly have been a catastrophe.'

No, but it would have given her a day's breathing-space to get used to the arrangements he'd made without consulting her! Her irritation at his lack of consideration subsided as genuine excitement thrilled through her veins at the prospect of seeing for herself the scenes of Amélie's childhood which had been so often described to her—the majesty of the mountains, the scent of the maquis, the olive groves ...

'You know the island well?' Moving a little awkwardly as his eyes followed her round the room, she heaved out her suitcase from its position at the bottom of her wardrobe.

It was only marginally larger than a weekend bag so perhaps it was just as well he wasn't taking her to a smart resort! A tendril of blonde hair fell forward over her cheek and she brushed it back with an impatient hand.

'Well enough, but not intimately—an omission I hope to put right in time.'

Sensitive to the hint of regret in his voice, Aphra paused in her task, turning her head so that she could read his withdrawn expression as he continued bleakly, 'I expect my grandmother told you that she never returned to her own country after her marriage to my grandfather, but that she'd always hoped that one day my father would go back to visit the village where she was born.'

'She told me she'd never recovered from his death.' Neatly Aphra folded a pair of jeans, bedding them down on top of the small pile of underwear she'd already placed in the case, before returning to the wardrobe, determined to make her own choice as to what was most suitable for the days ahead, and deciding to add a cotton skirt and a summer dress as well as a pair of lightweight sandals to the list Luc had prescribed.

'I know.' His voice was taut with pain. 'She used to tell me that losing a husband was a tragedy, but that losing a child was the greatest catastrophe which could befall a woman.'

And for a young child to lose both his parents? A fierce pain tugged at Aphra's heart as she tried to imagine the reaction of the orphaned five-year-old Luc to the realisation that he would never see his mother or father again.

'But she had you,' she pointed out carefully, pausing in her packing so that she could meet the fierce sorrow in his eyes, her compassion wrenched by the barely hidden anguish she'd detected in his tone. 'At least she had you, Luc—someone to continue living for—'

'Someone whose final neglect became the reason for her death? Is that what you're saying, Aphra?' Harshly he threw the words at her. 'You believe it was my absence, my lack of communication which brought on her final stroke, don't you?'

'Luc—no!' She'd meant to console him, not condemn him. Horrified, she stared at the torment reflected on his prepossessing face. 'Of course she missed you; I can't deny that. But she never doubted you would return to Fairmead eventually. She was looking forward to seeing you again—'

'And grew tired of waiting?' The question was obviously rhetorical, as he continued without pause, 'She'd lost her husband, her son, and now her grandson had disappeared off the face of the earth. Her reason for living was no longer valid, hmm?'

He came towards her, proud in his self-recrimination, seizing her by both arms, forcing her to gaze up into the bottomless depths of his haunted eyes. 'Oh, it wouldn't stand up in a court of law, but that doesn't worry you, does it? You tried and condemned me on hearsay without even trying to discover if there were any mitigating circumstances.'

It wasn't true! Yes, at the time she'd been angry about his continued silence. But she'd known too much about the unpredictability of strokes to lay Amélie's death at his door. Besides, she *knew* the mitigating circumstances. He'd told her about them himself, and, no stranger to emotional pain, she understood how Kathryn's departure from his life must have affected him.

There was a moment's tense silence as she found her larynx stilled by nerves. Then a great wave of sympathy for his anguish stirred in her heart, accompanied by something more frightening still—a wayward desire to comfort him with her own body, to receive the domination of his mouth, and in some way to alleviate his agony by taking it from him, absorbing it into her own tissues.

'Luc—it wasn't like that.' She scanned his troubled face for signs that she could penetrate the hard shell of his pain. Behind the façade of the adult man she sensed the scars of the five-year-old boy whose parents had left him for the first time in his short life to go on a business trip to Switzerland, and had lost their lives when a cable-car had fallen from its heights into the icy cavern beneath it, leaving no survivors.

'Tell me . . .' His fingers travelled in slow, hypnotic movements against the silk of her jacket. 'Since you set yourself up as such an expert in love, tell me what losing someone you love is like. Tell me how you go on living when you can't cast their memory from your mind yet you can't reach out and touch them. Does it get better in time? Or do you find a substitute lover and close your eyes when you kiss so that you can conjure up the face and taste of your beloved?'

'Luc, please . . . I thought we were talking about Amélie . . .' Suddenly Aphra's throat was parched, as the phantom laughter of Kathryn Bellini seemed to echo at her from every corner of the room.

'Wrong, Aphra. I was talking about love. The kind of love which manifests itself like this . . .'

Before she could prevent him Luc had drawn her unsuspecting body firmly into his embrace, lowering his head to possess her mouth as she struggled instinctively to escape the pressure of his hard masculinity against her unyielding flesh.

Totally unprepared for his sensual assault, she gave a small cry, half-surprised, half-protesting, as his lips left hers to travel a passionate path down her throat, leaning backwards against the powerful support of his arms.

When his mouth continued its path to nuzzle the hollow between her collar-bones, she closed her eyes, allowing her senses to flood with the pleasure of his nearness, every nerve centre recording its delight at the scent and substance of his taut skin and soft, thick hair.

Caught in the magic of a sensual experience she'd never known before, she was suddenly no longer straining against the imprisonment of his arms but remaining motionless, her head flung back, her hair streaming down her back as a tide of longing flowed through her blood.

Only when she felt his warm, seeking mouth caress the taut peak of one breast did she realise that Luc had slipped one adventurous hand inside the soft fabric of her blouse in order to capture and enjoy this intimate part of her body.

'Luc! No!' Disturbed as much by her own response as by his unexpected and passionate invasion of her personal privacy, she reared away from him, covering her exposed flesh with a hand which trembled. How could she behave so brazenly when she knew how deeply he despised her?

His face was devoid of expression, a hard, beautiful mask, as he gazed at her troubled countenance. Only the harsh sound of his breathing demonstrated the degree of his leashed arousal.

'You're right,' he said tautly. 'This is neither the time nor place. We have a plane to catch. Half an hour, then, Aphra. Please don't keep me waiting. I'll be downstairs with our guests.'

Still in a daze, she watched him move towards the door, conscious only of the wild hammering of her heart allied to a deep apprehension.

On the threshold he paused, turning to regard her thoughtfully. For a brief moment she found herself hoping for some word of encouragement, anything to suggest that what he had just done had not been entirely due to his fixation with his lost love, then the door was closing behind him and she was alone with her half-packed suitcase and a feeling of utter desolation.

CHAPTER SIX

FAR below her, a river gleamed like a ribbon of molten metal as the rays of the late afternoon sun reflected from its calm surface. No stranger to flying, Aphra relaxed in her luxurious seat, staring out at the passing landscape, recalling her shocked reaction when she'd realised that the small jet primed and ready for take-off at the privately owned airport was intended for just her and her husband.

'You told Liz you weren't using a company plane!' she'd exclaimed in surprise.

'Neither am I.' Luc's tone had been impatient. 'This one is privately hired, out of my own pocket. There weren't any scheduled direct flights from the south of England to Corsica, and I wasn't in the mood to break our journey in Paris. Another time, perhaps—but not now. Is it important, Aphra?'

'No, of course not,' she'd said quietly, hurt by the asperity in his tone. She hadn't expected him to keep up the act of enamoured bridegroom once they were free of the Hall and its happy temporary occupants, but she'd hoped they might find a platform of friendship on which to meet. Instead, all she had been able to sense was Luc's hostility pricking at her sensitive skin like ice shards.

'Are you going to pilot it yourself?' she'd enquired sweetly, directly provocative as her innocent gaze had panned his set face.

'Sorry to disappoint you, darling. Aviation isn't amongst my many talents, and, even if it were, as a newly-wed man I'd prefer to spend the flight with my wife rather than at the controls of an aeroplane.'

Many talents indeed! She'd turned her head from his bland expression and without another word ascended the small flight of steps to the main cabin, temporarily forgetting her chagrin as she'd been greeted by a smiling hostess and led into the body of the plane, which had been transformed into a comfortable sitting room.

She'd been suitably impressed, a small smile lifting the corners of her mouth as she'd thought of her parents. No strangers to first-class travel, even they, she'd suspected, had never flown in such luxury!

Luc sat, his long legs stretched out in the comfortable space, his gaze fixed on the pages of the current edition of the *Wall Street Journal*, which he'd chosen from the on-board selection of newspapers.

He must be finding its contents extraordinarily interesting, she thought bleakly as the coast of France disappeared in the distance beneath her, since it had occupied his attention exclusively from the moment he'd first opened it.

Staring covertly at his stern features as he lounged in the seat opposite her, Aphra felt her apprehension deepen. How had she ever deceived herself into believing that this man had played any role in her earlier life? His presence on the stage during some of the scenes of her adolescence had been purely coincidental; the warmth in her heart from the glow of his personality a mere by-product of a charisma of youth and achievement so powerful that it had reached unwittingly and unknowingly into her innocent soul.

How disastrously she'd fooled herself! Right up to the moment of signing the register, she'd hoped subconsciously that despite the uneasiness of their encounter in the garden they could learn to tolerate each other's presence; that their joint interests in preserving Fairmead would serve as a solid basis for the lifestyle they would be obliged to formulate and act out in the months ahead.

But being married to Luc was going to be a lot worse than she'd anticipated, she realised forlornly, because he neither liked nor respected her. In fact, since the ceremony he seemed as if he could barely endure her presence.

It was the appearance of the stewardess with a menu in her hand which brought her back to the present with a small start of surprise.

'But I've been eating all afternoon!' she protested laughingly as she accepted the card. 'I'm not sure I've room for anything else.'

'I'd advise you to try at least,' Luc suggested smoothly. 'It's the last meal you're likely to get before breakfast tomorrow. 'We've a long drive ahead of us after we land at Ajaccio, and Amélie's old home doesn't possess the luxury of a freezer — or a refrigerator, for that matter, so your access to food will be limited until the morning when the shops open.'

'It sounds delightful.' Irritated more by his tone than the contents of his message, she raised her eyebrows in mock disapproval. 'I take it there's fresh water available in case I feel thirsty?'

'There's a pump in the garden.' Luc nodded, his gaze complacent. 'I'm afraid that you're going to be disillusioned if you were expecting all modern conveniences. The village is well off the beaten tourist track, although some valiant hikers manage to find it. It's what optimists call "unspoiled".'

'And pessimists "primitive"?' she challenged, annoyed by the provocative look in his dark eyes. 'I wasn't expecting the Hilton!'

'Then you won't be disappointed.'

There was a quiet sense of satisfaction in his tone which puzzled her.

'What made you think I might be?' she queried, her eyebrows lifting slightly as she met his unforthcoming expression. 'Have you forgotten I spent a large part of my childhood living in the country?'

'No.' His smile was enigmatic. 'As a matter of fact I've been remembering a few more episodes where our paths crossed in the past. Tell me, Aphra—' he leant towards her confidentially '—what were you running away from when you decided to bury yourself in Leamarsh again?'

'Nothing that need concern you, Luc,' she returned tartly, determined not to submit herself to a cross-examination. 'We have a business relationship which doesn't give you the right to pry into my personal affairs.'

'And how many of those have you had, I wonder?' He regarded her unresponsive face contemplatively. 'Well, however many there may have been in the past, there aren't going to be any in the foreseeable future, I can assure you. You may see our relationship as a purely business one, but as far as I'm concerned I expect a great deal more from you than I would from a paid employee, and the sooner you understand that, the better it will be for you!'

'Are you threatening me, Luc?' she queried quietly, hoping she had successfully masked the wave of apprehension which had surged through her.

'Warning, not threatening—and only in respect of your future financial well-being.' He gave her a thin, dangerous smile, which suggested that he wasn't unaware of her inner alarm. 'I've never laid a finger on a woman yet unless she invited it—and then only to please her.'

For a fraction of a second the emotional adolescent lying dormant inside Aphra seemed to surface as she envisaged with embarrassing clarity just how satisfying it would be for a woman to be pleasured by Luc Benchard. The absurd picture sent an humiliating warmth to her cheeks—a colour which deepened with anger as he added curtly, 'However devious your motives are for enabling me to save Fairmead from demolition, one thing is beyond doubt. You are now my wife, and, like Caesar's, I expect you to be above suspicion.'

'Wife, Luc?' Her eyes sparkled with antagonism. 'No, you're wrong. I'm not your wife. I'm your obligatory bride—and the rules aren't the same!'

'Not so, my darling.' Luc's deep tones corrected her with the speed of a lizard's tongue seizing its prey, but the gentle curl of his tender mouth was not echoed in the cool stare from his sombre eyes. 'The rules are mine to make and yours to obey. That way there'll be no tears.'

'Ah, but hadn't you heard? It's officially all right for macho men to weep now. In fact some women find it very attractive.' Shocked by his unexpected display of male chauvinism, she kept her voice light, choosing deliberately to misunderstand him.

'Unfortunately I can't say I feel the same way about women's tears,' he returned pleasantly. 'I find little attraction in swollen eyes and mascara-streaked cheeks.'

'Then I pity you, Luc,' she said quietly, deciding to ignore the implicit caution his words contained. 'Because a man without compassion is like an egg without a yolk.'

The simile surprised her as much as it apparently astonished her argumentative spouse if the quick flicker of his sumptuous eyelashes was anything to go by, Aphra observed, feeling a quiet glow of satisfaction warm her.

Strange, but she'd never considered herself particularly expert in repartee, yet the words had sprung to her tongue with a speed which suggested they'd been rehearsed.

'You believe I don't possess a soft centre?' he returned silkily.

An irrational urge to flirt with him in the confined safety of the aeroplane assailed her. 'Do you?' she asked, deliberately batting her eyelashes at him. 'Oh, I do hope so, Luc! I've always had a weakness for a soft centre.'

'I'm delighted to hear it, Aphra.'

She found the cool laughter in his eyes disquieting. Heaven only knew what the stewardess thought of their strange conversation. But a quick glance confirmed that the other woman had discreetly withdrawn to await their summons, as Luc continued smoothly, 'I was beginning to think that you were made entirely of steel from the crown of your lovely blonde head to the soles of your expensive shoes. To learn that you've got at least one vulnerable spot is good news indeed. Perhaps, in time, I may even discover a few more.'

Before she could determine his purpose, he'd reached easily across the table which separated them to slide one hand against her body beneath the cover of her jacket and imprison the swell of her breast.

So close to him that she could read the cool contempt in the dark eyes which assessed her reaction, Aphra felt a small pulse begin to beat quickly in the hollow of her throat.

A muffled cry, half of pleasure, half of protest, burst from her lips as the warmth of his fingers pierced the light bodyshaper and gauzy blouse which covered her skin, and she was forced to acknowledge the sensual power he could wield over her.

What she would have done next she would never know, because Luc withdrew his hand with contemptuous ease, using it to indicate the discarded menu.

'Better make the most of civilisation while it lasts.'

She did—not so much in obedience to Luc's command, but because she judged that the act of eating would make the probability of further disquieting conversation less likely.

The simmering tension she felt was not conducive to a good appetite, and she only picked at the country paté served with thin slivers of buttered toast, followed by crispy duck in orange sauce with wild rice. If it hadn't been for several glasses of a classic white Burgundy she doubted if she could have swallowed more than a couple of mouthfuls of food. But she welcomed the final course of *crème caramel* and the aromatic black coffee which followed it.

It was as if something had happened within the last few hours to change Luc's attitude towards her. She twisted her new wedding ring thoughtfully. She'd supposed that their mutual understanding would have dulled the edge of the antagonism which had flared between them at their first meeting in the garden. Instead, since the wedding ceremony, the atmosphere between them had deteriorated even further.

It didn't augur well for the future, she thought disconsolately, especially since she was becoming more and more aware of the fact that although Luc still mourned the loss of Kathryn his appetite for sensual pleasure had in no way abated.

Worse still, she was forced to admit that the hero-worship she had once felt for him seemed to have been replaced by some other emotion which was far more uncomfortable and potentially dangerous. Why else should she have responded so readily to his touch, the feel of his hand against her breast?

Stirring restlessly in her comfortable seat, she was bitterly aware, too, that since the simple ceremony which had bound them as man and wife Luc's attitude towards her had hardened even more than she had anticipated.

She was still trying to come to terms with her ambivalent feelings when the plane came in to land at Ajaccio.

Despite the strained circumstances of her visit she felt a rising tide of excitement when she stepped onto Corsican soil as the last rays of the sun disappeared below the horizon.

'Where to now?' She'd waited until they'd accomplished the fast and simple process of passing through Immigration Control before posing the question.

'North towards Porto and east towards the mountains. There should be transport waiting.'

There was. An ancient Land Rover with dust-stained sides.

'Don't be put off by the bodywork.' Luc swung her case into the back of the vehicle. 'I can assure you it's mechanically sound and perfectly suited to the terrain.'

'Well, that's a relief.' She climbed into the front passenger seat as Luc tossed his jacket into the back together with his tie and loosened his shirt at the collar before easing himself behind the wheel. 'I wouldn't want to break down in the middle of nowhere and have to walk.'

'You won't.' His lips parted in a brief smile. 'You can rely on me to get you there safely. I'm no stranger to the route.'

It would be a brave vehicle which dared to label him a liar, Aphra thought wryly, settling back in her seat, content to lapse into silence as they started on their journey.

She'd had no intention of sleeping, so it must have been the motion of the vehicle plus the surrounding darkness of the warm, velvet evening allied to the exhausting nervous tension which had plagued her all day which acted as a soporific, because the next thing she knew was that the car had stopped and Luc was gently shaking her shoulder.

'Welcome to my other ancestral home, Aphra.'

'Have we arrived?' She stumbled out of the open door, not surprised when she didn't receive an answer to her rhetorical question. Blinking in the darkness, her senses assailed by an assortment of perfumes, she found herself facing the entrance to an old stone-built cottage.

'This is it?' She peered at the flaking white paint as her eyes became accustomed to the moonlight which bathed the scene, her glance encompassing the old wooden shutters, once painted blue but now sun-bleached and peeling.

'Quite a change from Fairmead Hall, yes?' There was a note of quiet triumph in Luc's voice as he took her arm, leading her firmly towards the solid wooden door. 'Of course, it's been modernised since the time Amélie and my grandfather met, especially the interior.' Producing a large key, he thrust it in the lock, opening the door and standing back to allow Aphra to cross the threshold first. 'Today it's owned by a holiday company and let out to people who prefer the beauty of the mountains to the heat of the beaches—hunters, walkers, people who enjoy solitude.'

'Honeymoon couples?' she enquired drily as an unshaded bulb sprang into life, illuminating a bare lobby containing a rack of hooks nailed to the wall above a narrow shelf, and an empty stand presumably meant for walking sticks—or rifles? After all, he had said something about hunting.

'Why not?' He discounted her irony with a lofty wave of his hand. 'It has everything that two lovers could possibly need—isolation, peace and a view to awaken and rejuvenate the senses when they are replete. What more could anyone ask?'

'A maid service and a good restaurant?' Aphra countered, wondering what sight would meet her eyes as Luc opened the only other door that led from the lobby. She was pleasantly surprised as a centre light, covered this time with an amber shade, sprang to life. The room was much larger than she'd anticipated.

The white-painted walls were in good repair, the tiled floor bore two large woven rugs, whilst an assortment of dark wooden furniture, the chairs comfortably upholstered with cushions, was distributed in a pleasing arrangement. The dark wood motif was continued in the number of shelves bearing brightly coloured ceramic plates and other bits and pieces that she would be interested to examine at a later time.

'And this is the bedroom.' Luc had moved to one of the doors at the further end of the room while her gaze had been elsewhere. Again he stood back to allow her first access.

Even before she'd crossed the living room to accept his invitation she'd known from the expression on his face what awaited her. Simplicity was still the keyword. A large chest of drawers, a smaller one with a mirror placed over it, a large wardrobe and there, in pride of place, an old-fashioned double bed, covered by an entirely up-to-date rose-printed duvet.

'Is this the only bedroom?' she asked levelly, already anticipating his reply.

'Yes.' Expressionless eyes scrutinised her coolly. 'Why?'

The mockery in his voice seared her as she took a deep breath in an effort to quieten the sudden increased rate of her heartbeat. Luc had never given her an explicit undertaking that they should have separate rooms—but surely it had been a mutual understanding? Hadn't he suggested as much when he'd given her the reason for their not remaining at Fairmead?

'This morning's ceremony was for legal not personal reasons, as you're well aware,' she countered evenly. 'There was never any suggestion that we—we should sleep together.'

'What a quaint expression! Now, what exactly do you mean by it, I wonder?' His dark eyes, alight and gleaming, assessed her embarrassment. 'Are you referring to sharing a bed or indulging in a much more intimate entertainment?'

'Both,' she returned bleakly. 'I expected to have my own room as well as my own bed.'

Luc shrugged his broad shoulders. 'Tough luck, darling.' He regarded her with scant sympathy. 'But, if it makes you feel any happier, it's been a challenging day for me too. I've no intention of claiming my marital rights tonight.'

Resolutely banishing to the back of her mind the mixed emotions she'd felt beneath the careless and disdainful caresses he'd bestowed on her throughout the day, she began angrily, 'You don't have any rights—'

'Also—' Luc brushed away her protest with the same nonchalance as he might have brushed an insect from his sleeve '—if it's any consolation to you I understand that I don't snore and I'm not a restless sleeper. In fact, as bedmates go, I've been told I'm gold-medal standard.'

'The point is,' Aphra returned furiously, 'I'm used to sleeping alone.'

She hesitated, wondering if it was advisable or even possible to explain to him how deeply she feared the resulting loss of personal space, the intimacy of lying semi-clothed and unconscious near his alien body, flesh touching flesh unknowingly in the small, dark hours of the morning.

'How very enlightening.' Luc's eyes were bright with an emotion she couldn't translate. 'Perhaps if your ex-husband had been less considerate of your whims and foibles your first marriage would have lasted a little longer than it did, hmm?' He eyed her speculatively, challengingly.

Belatedly she realised her mistake in not having told him the truth about her marriage to Peter. If she hadn't been so angry at his baseless assumptions about her character—or rather lack of it—and if there'd been more time before their hurried wedding then she probably would have done. Not that she had anticipated the present scenario!

When she'd considered their life post-wedding, she'd seen herself living at Fairmead as Luc's nominal wife as well as continuing the career for which she'd been trained, whilst Luc stayed at his London apartment, perhaps commuting at the weekend... Now she was beginning to feel less and less sanguine about his plans for the months ahead.

'Peter... Peter and I...' she began, panic squeezing her throat, so that the words came out thin and breathy as she tried to rearrange her thoughts into a logical sequence.

'Yes?' Dark eyebrows lifted slightly as Luc raised a hand to the lintel of the door, propping himself up and staring down into her face with an air of polite enquiry which didn't fool her for one moment. Something was eating at him—something which was raising his antagonism towards her by the moment.

'Tell me about Peter and you.' The seductive timbre of his voice was pleasant yet to Aphra's sensitive ears it held some kind of threat she couldn't understand.

'Although what Peter and I had just didn't last, I can assure you that the question of sharing a bed wasn't a factor in our—our final separation,' she informed him tightly.

'So what was, hmm?'

Pushing himself abruptly away from the door-frame, he walked into the room, his fingers tearing at his shirt buttons, wrenching them through the holes with a mean purpose. 'After all, husbands and wives should have no secrets, and you know all about my beautiful Kathryn and how she walked out on me. So tell me, what caused the break-up of love's young dream? Was he unfaithful? Or did he neglect you? Or perhaps you were the one who wandered. Is that it, Aphra? I think you owe me an explanation, don't you?'

He shrugged the shirt from his back, flinging it across the room, so that it caught at the edge of the chest of drawers before tumbling to the floor. Turning back, he captured her gaze, compelling Aphra's breath to catch in her throat as the vision of his semi-nakedness startled her into silence.

It wasn't the first time she'd seen him stripped to the waist, or thrilled to the sheer perfection of his muscle-toughened shoulders and washboard abdomen. But then she'd been younger. Too young to respond with the singing physical thrill which now tingled through every cell of her body.

Then she'd been a child, innocently admiring the taut yet flexible frame of a young athlete who with typically male unselfconsciousness had sometimes wandered from the changing room into the main hall of the pavilion before donning his non-strip T-shirt.

'I owe you nothing!'

With an effort she banned the intrusive picture, angry that she'd even allowed it to linger for that brief second. What good would the truth do now anyway? The last thing she needed was Luc's pity—not that even that would be forthcoming if she was reading the sardonic look on his face correctly.

Ridicule, then? Much more likely, she decided numbly. His continual sarcastic usage of the endearment 'darling' since the wedding ceremony hadn't escaped her. She certainly had no intention of exposing Peter's memory to his further scorn.

Her emotions rising in an angry spiral of pain and mortification, she faced up to him challengingly. 'You've no right whatsoever to question me about my past. It should be enough that I helped you fulfil Amélie's last wishes.'

'You had your own motives.' Dourly he regarded her pale face and taut stance. 'If you're expecting me to go down on my knees in gratitude in return for your complicity, forget it! Besides, it's early days yet. You've still got a lot to learn if you're to give a convincing performance when we go back to Leamarsh. That's another reason I brought you here. Without the interruption of well-wishers there'll be plenty of time for me to teach you how to behave yourself before letting you loose on my friends and colleagues.'

'You have problems with my manners?' she demanded, astounded, her voice rising querulously. 'Let me tell you, I went to—'

She'd been going to say 'one of the best and most famous girls' boarding-schools in the country', but fortunately he forestalled her—fortunately, because he would never have believed that little Annie Glover had been allowed over the threshold of such an august institution, and she was in no mood to attempt a substantiation of her claim tonight.

'Not your manners, your attitude.' He gave an impatient shrug. 'Sleep on the couch if you want to, but there's only one duvet and the early hours before dawn tend to be cold at this time of the year.' An impatient breath emphasised his irritation. 'Look, Aphra, I've told you my plans for tonight don't include an attempt at seduction.'

'That's lucky for you,' she flashed back. 'Because it would have been doomed to failure.'

Her heart pounding with mixed emotions, she cast a critical look at the bed. If she wanted a comfortable night's rest she was going to have to yield her position, and with as much dignity as possible.

Moving further into the room, she tested the resilience of the mattress, finding it firm but springy. 'All right, Luc,' she said coolly, 'since I have your word that you won't molest me, I'll share with you tonight, but unfortunately I can't provide any testimonials about my sleeping habits. If my snoring keeps you awake, or your dreams are disturbed by an unfriendly knee in your groin, you'll have only yourself to blame.'

Her small chin rose sharply as she discerned a gleam of laughter in his insolent eyes. She hadn't meant to amuse him. 'Perhaps you'll be good enough to show me where the water supply is—and the usual toilet facilities.'

Anticipating an excursion into the garden as she recalled his comments about the pump, she was astonished when he informed her politely, 'You passed the door to the bathroom on your way here.'

Scarcely daring to believe that he was telling her the truth, she grabbed her case and took it with her to the door they had passed on their way to the bedroom. Half expecting it would lead directly to some unfriendly terrain at the back of the cottage, she was greatly relieved to find that the small room beyond it had been modernised and contained adequate sanitary provision, including a shower.

At this time of night all she wanted to do was wash her face and clean her teeth. Stripping down to her undies in the narrow confines of the room, she ignored the simple cotton nightdress she'd packed when under the impression she'd be spending the night on her own, choosing instead to clamber into a pair of well-worn cotton jeans covered by a T-shirt.

It wasn't that she didn't trust Luc to keep his word, she told herself, just that she assessed him to be a young and virile man with powerful appetites—the kind of man who would not need love as a stimulant for sexual release.

He might neither like nor admire her. He might, in fact, actively dislike what he perceived to be her character, but she'd be a fool to ignore the sparks which burned between them every time he laid a finger on her body, or the treacherous surge of pleasure which invaded her senses at his insolent touch.

Luc, too, was aware of the unwelcome chemistry which flared between them. She was sure of it. Why else would the pressure of his fingers on her skin sear her as much by its disdain as by its contained animal passion?

She shivered. Whatever satisfaction the physical act of union with Luc might bring her, and she was honest enough to acknowledge a growing awareness in every cell of her body that the pleasure involved could be mind-shattering, she would never be able to live with the humiliation of knowing that her flesh had been a poor substitute for that of the faithless Kathryn.

Tomorrow she must make her position totally clear to him. In the meantime the least she could do was ensure that her nightwear gave out no contrary message about the strength of her own resolution to keep him at arm's length.

CHAPTER SEVEN

SUNLIGHT was streaming in through the shutters when Aphra awakened, to an atmosphere heavy with the scent of freshly brewed coffee. Somewhere a donkey brayed as she pulled herself upright, disentangling her legs from the crumpled duvet which, at some time earlier, she must have relegated to waist-level.

Of Luc there was no sign, she realised with relief. She must have fallen asleep as soon as her head had touched the comfortable pillow because all she could recall was the wryly sardonic twist of Luc's mouth as she'd reappeared in the bedroom in her selected nightwear.

Swinging her jeans-clad legs out of bed, she acknowledged ruefully that they weren't the most comfortable garments in which to sleep. The T-shirt alone would have been more suitable. It might also have been misinterpreted, giving a message to Luc that she'd had no intention of sending.

Not that she found him physically unappealing, she admitted ruefully—quite the opposite in fact, and therein lay the danger. Just suppose he hadn't been simply trying to annoy her by claiming that physical intimacy within their marriage hadn't been precluded?

An inner restlessness plucked at her nervous system, forcing her to admit that deep within her lay a hunger which was crying out to be satiated in Luc's arms, satisfied beneath his powerful body. Angrily, she tried to force the realisation from her mind. Without emotional rapport, pure physical enjoyment would surely be a brief and empty pleasure, wouldn't it—leaving behind a pain far worse than the one it temporarily relieved?

Whatever role Luc might have in mind for her, it certainly would not include temporarily understudying the star part of the faithless Kathryn, she determined stormily. If he truly wasn't aware of that fact, then the sooner she made that absolutely plain the better!

There was no sign of Luc in the living room either, but a large ceramic jug on top of a small portable hotplate standing on a heavily carved sideboard proved to be the source of the coffee smell. Gratefully she poured herself a fragrant mugful, taking it into the bathroom with her, together with a change of clothes. Glad to find a substantial bolt on the door, she stripped off, gratified to discover that the water from the shower was pleasingly warm. Presumably the hardy walkers and hunters were not immune to a desire for their own creature comforts!

Twenty minutes later she felt fit to face the world—or at least the part of it outside the cottage door. Dressed in a clean pair of jeans and a short-sleeved cotton top, her hair brushed into a shining pony-tail neatly anchored with a tortoiseshell slide, she padded towards the main door on comfortably soled deck-shoes, and threw it open, catching her breath in instinctive awe at the scene before her.

The previous night it had been too dark and she'd been too exhausted even to attempt to discern the cottage's surroundings. Now the landscape was of a rose-flushed mountain valley blooming beneath towering mountain peaks still bespattered with gleaming snow. In the clear air, far above her head, a pair of eagles wheeled, superb in their powerful beauty.

So this had been Amélie's home village—this huddle of stone-built cottages perched between the mountain-pierced sky and the tumbling foothills which were spewed out beneath her, their fertile soil hosting groves of orange and olive trees.

Somewhere far below she thought she caught the sparkle of water, and recalled that the island had many rivers which tumbled their way from the high mountains to the resorts along the popular Mediterranean coastline.

Carefully she took stock of the immediate surroundings. It seemed that Amélie's cottage was on the outskirts of the village, separate from the cluster of similar terracotta-roofed buildings which clung to the ascending mountainside, the only access to which appeared to be by way of a dusty, stone-strewn path more suitable for use by the four feet of a donkey than four wheels!

Reluctantly she forced her eyes away from the magnificent view, turning instead to look at the cottage itself. In the clear mountain air, she saw that it possessed a sense of rightness, that the modernisations had been done with understanding and affection, so that the exterior still blended in with the scenery.

Curiosity took her through the short, dry grass at the side of the building to the plot at the back. Here nature had been left to do its own thing and had obliged by providing a thatch of sweet-scented golden-yellow gorse, well past the best of its flowering, she supposed, but still attracting a dusting of bees.

Neither had Luc been lying when he'd said there was a pump in the garden! Heaven knew how old it was but, from the appearance of the bucket and the dampness of the stone on which it stood, it was still functional.

Closing her eyes, she inhaled the sweet, potent scent which permeated the atmosphere. Now she understood Amélie's insistence on planting the highly scented shrubs at Fairmead Hall, and her cultivation of a herb garden.

Familiar perfumes crowded Aphra as she stood, her hands clasped loosely in front of her, her face turned towards the early sunshine, recognising old friends. Rosemary and oregano, the sharpness of lemon balm and the insidious, pungent scent of mint...

'Daydreaming, Aphrodite?'

Luc's softly spoken question brought her sharply back to reality as she opened her eyes with a start of surprise.

'I didn't hear you come!' It was part explanation, part reproach because he had interrupted an idyll of almost hypnotic intensity, and for a moment she resented his intrusion.

His dark eyebrows rose questioningly above his cool gaze as it met her veiled hostility. 'I took a stroll to the local *boulangerie*. I thought you might appreciate some breakfast.'

He was carrying a paper bag from which protruded a baguette, the aroma of which mingled with the other perfumes to awaken the realisation that she was indeed hungry—not to say ravenous.

'Yes, I would.' She proffered an awkward smile, every nerve of her body on edge. Until Luc had appeared on the scene, she'd been relaxed. Now she felt ill at ease—like an actress cast into a part she hadn't even read.

He turned abruptly and she followed him, aware of an odd emptiness, a different kind of hunger somewhere in the region of her solar plexus. How could she not be aware of the power of the lithe male body which preceded her?

How could she deny the magnetism he still exercised over her, or fail to be moved by the beauty of his dark hair burnished by sunlight, the strength of his wide shoulders beneath the light blue cotton of his T-shirt or the hidden power of his formidable legs beneath the dark denim which clung to them?

Last night she'd slept beside him, her body and spirit exhausted, confident that he wouldn't touch her without her consent. And her confidence had been justified. But suppose in the coming days he canvassed that consent—not because he cared for her, but as a casual relief for the building tensions in his virile male body?

With a sinking feeling of despair at her own vulnerability, she admitted that, despite her recent resolution, she could not guarantee that she would be able to repulse him.

* * *

'Did Amélie ever tell you how she came to marry my grandfather?'

Hours later Aphra was relaxing on a bed of pine needles in the welcome shade of a small forest, narrowing her eyes as she stared at the glistening sea visible far below between the tall, straight trunks, when Luc asked her the question.

It had been he who, after breakfast, had proposed the walk, suggesting it wasn't too strenuous for her first day. It had been he, too, who had organised and carried a picnic lunch, which he'd laid out at her feet when the time had come for rest.

Freshly baked bread, slices of cold pork, soft *brocciu* cheese made from ewes' milk and seasoned with the aromatic herbs of the maquis and, to follow, fat red cherries the size of small plums and slices of delicious chestnut cake. Still mineral water and a dry white wine from Porto Vecchio, carefully packed in cool-bags, had accompanied one of the most enjoyable meals she'd ever eaten.

It had been a silent walk, each of them seemingly immersed in his and her own thoughts. Silent, but not uncomfortably so, Aphra decided, sneaking a glance at Luc's prepossessing profile as he lounged beside her as if he had called a truce on their differences.

'Only that she was eighteen when they first met here in Corsica, that he was three years older than her and that it was love at first sight.' She smiled reminiscently. 'She said that the Benchards were furious when he arrived back in England with what they described as "a dark-haired, illiterate savage", and that his widowed father and younger brother never forgave him for introducing foreign blood into the family.' She sighed. 'It sounded such a romantic story.'

'Intriguing rather than romantic.' Amusement tinged the timbre of Luc's voice. 'At the time Amélie was already betrothed against her will to one of her distant cousins—a widower a great deal older than her with the added disadvantages of being fat, ugly and ill-tempered.'

'You mean she had no say in the matter?'

Luc uttered a brief, deprecatory laugh. 'Life in the early twentieth century wasn't particularly kind to working-class countrywomen in southern Europe, where the male head of household was usually dominant to the point of tyranny.

'But Amélie was bright and spirited enough to want to break free from a life of poverty, drudgery and endless childbearing tied to a man she neither liked nor admired, totally subjugated to his will. So when my grandfather and a couple of his friends stayed overnight at the local hostelry during a holiday in the mountains she saw her opportunity—and seized it.'

There was a spark of reluctant admiration in Luc's eyes as he paused, before continuing, 'Since, of the three men, she found my grandfather the most attractive, it was to him she went that night, tricking him by means of some incoherent message into meeting her outside the inn and throwing herself into his arms, but not before she'd made sure that the emotive little scene was witnessed by at least two of her brothers.'

'You mean she tried to compromise him?' Aphra demanded, astonished.

'And succeeded.' Luc nodded.

'But surely he protested his total innocence?' She stared back at him, amazed by the simplistic nature of the plot. 'I mean, he hadn't even spoken to her, had he?'

'No, he hadn't,' Luc agreed calmly. 'But despite his agonised denials they didn't believe him. So, faced with the alternatives of marriage to Amélie or being shot, he decided the former would be the more sensible choice.'

'Amélie was prepared to put her life into the hands of a complete stranger?' Disbelief echoed in Aphra's voice.

Luc nodded his dark head again. 'She might have been an ignorant peasant girl but she recognised quality of spirit when she saw it. She told me she fully expected my grandfather to get the marriage annulled once they were out of Corsica. After all, the union had been forced at gunpoint, and witnessed by two of his friends who would testify on his behalf, but in the meantime she trusted him to treat her with respect whilst she was in his custody.'

'I hadn't realised. She always gave me the impression that theirs was a great love match.' It was an idea she was still reluctant to abandon.

'So it was,' Luc affirmed gently. 'It just had a rather traumatic beginning. By the time Grandfather got her back to England he was totally besotted by his fiery Corsican bride.' He paused momentarily. 'And it's not just Amélie's word I have for that. With her blessing I've read the letters he sent to her from France during the Second World War. There's no doubt that he adored her.'

'But surely it was an empty threat her brothers made?' Aphra leant forward, clasping her hands round her knees, her eyes sparkling with interest. 'I mean, he must have known they wouldn't have killed him.'

'On the contrary. He was well informed. He knew they most certainly would.'

'But that would have been murder!' Horrified, she refused to believe him.

'So what?' Luc eased his position. 'Death was the price paid for dishonour in those days. Believe me, even now, it pays to treat a Corsican woman with respect. Even when the ultimate sentence wasn't passed, the punishment for seducing a local woman could be direfully and fittingly painful.

'Legend has it that the Roman philosopher Seneca, who was in exile here, made the bad mistake of seducing a shepherd's daughter and the even worse mistake of letting her brothers discover that he'd dishonoured her.'

'So they killed him?' Aphra raised astonished eyebrows.

'No,' Luc contradicted her cheerfully, 'they decided on a rather more lingering form of punishment. Arming themselves with a particularly vicious variety of stinging nettle, and having removed any protective clothing from what they identified as the offending parts of Seneca's person, they applied the nettles to them with much vigour.'

'Oh!' Rough justice indeed. Or had he just made the tale up to shock her? 'Am I expected to believe that?'

'Suit yourself.' His gaze taunted her indecision. 'But that particular species of nettle is known to this day as the *ortica di Seneca*. Grand-mère made sure I knew the legend before my first visit to the island as a teenager. I imagine she thought it would be a powerful deterrent against any unseemly behaviour on my part!'

'And was it?' Aphra's eyes sparkled with amusement as she challenged him.

'An unnecessary one.' His steady gaze held her captive. 'By that time mass tourism had reached the island and the less formal female visitors were laying out their wares on the beaches for all to see and bid for.'

Aphra stirred uneasily as a strange emotion akin to jealousy assailed her. 'How convenient for you. I suppose you took full advantage of the opportunities offered,' she retorted tartly.

'Most young men of my age would have done.' It was neither confirmation nor denial, but the sudden gleam in his obsidian eyes promised her trouble. 'Since you hold such a low opinion of my powers of self-denial, answer me this—do you seriously believe I intend to live a life of celibacy for the next two years?'

As if commanded by some unseen signal the lazy hum of the cicadas which had accompanied the conversation ceased, leaving the question hanging in an uncanny silence.

Aphra was suddenly, searingly aware of Luc's dangerous stillness, the powerful emanation of his sexuality, and felt herself trembling as an unexpected and unwelcome rush of excitement flowed through her body.

One moment they'd been sharing the peace and beauty of the forest like friends—the next he'd introduced a carping note of dissent into the idyll. How foolish she'd been not to realise that he'd planned this confrontation from the start.

'No, of course I don't!' Resentment stiffened the tone of her voice. 'As far as I'm concerned you can be as promiscuous as you like with whom you like. I promise Leonard won't hear any complaints from me!'

'So you've had a change of heart?' The question was rhetorical as Luc continued glibly, 'You'll never know how happy I am to hear that.'

Realising too late that he had deliberately misconstrued her answer, Aphra opened her mouth to remonstrate, but before she could put her thoughts into words, Luc reached towards her, taking her by the shoulders and pushing her down onto the bed of pine needles as he covered her with his lean and powerful body, so that every curve and hollow she possessed was achingly aware of his masculine presence.

Even if she'd been prepared for the assault she couldn't have prevented it, because her own body was betraying her, moulding itself to receive him as shock waves of desire shuddered through every cell.

Mentally she was aware of an element of scorn in the way he was exercising his physical power over her, but as her heart thundered beneath his she found it impossible to deny him the possession of her mouth.

Closing her eyes, she accepted the smouldering power of his lips, responding intuitively, unquestioningly to a conquering force that she had no will to repel. It was impossible to hide her feelings; her breath caught in her throat in a deep sob of surrender.

'Who are you thinking of, Aphra?' Luc's voice was rough, vibrating with some kind of taut emotion that she had no chance of identifying let alone understanding, as his warm fingers slid into the simple V neckline of her casual cotton top, his acute gaze narrowed on her flushed face as she strove to escape from the hard pressure of his thighs weighing down on her own.

'Does it matter?' she asked shakily, her heart thundering beneath his hand as it moved with slow deliberation over her lace-covered breasts, caressing them with a lover's tenderness headily mixed with a seducer's guile.

What did he expect—a confession that her feelings towards him were warmer than she had ever acknowledged—even to herself? Dear heavens! Did he want to humiliate her in return for the sweetness of his caresses?

'Not any more...' His tone was velvet, edged with steel. 'Because I mean to wipe the names of your past lovers—whoever they were—from your memory, so that the only image to fill your mind as you take your pleasure from my body will be of me.' His breathing was laboured in the magical silence of the quivering warmth of the afternoon. 'And I do please you, do I not, sweet Aphra?'

Hopelessly aware of her own vulnerability, Aphra gathered her weakening defences. If she had any pride she'd struggle, oppose his male greed with female determination—and he would obey her. If she hadn't believed that, she would never have agreed to this unholy alliance.

She only had to reinforce her determination of not being his wife in anything but name and he would roll away from her, give her back her sovereignty over her body...

'No...no...' The half-hearted words of denial died on her tongue as the slow spiral of awareness he had conjured up in her tortured body swirled into an aching vortex of mindless pleasure. 'Luc...' She breathed his name, some distant part of her mind aware that his marauding hand had dropped to her waist as his dark, hypnotic eyes held her spellbound.

It was the sensation of his warm fingers against the bare skin of her midriff which shocked her back into reality. 'This isn't right!' she protested, despair and anger uniting in the huskiness of her voice as she attempted vainly to dislodge his hand.

'I'm not truly your wife, Luc. I'm your accomplice and the rules are different!' Uncertainly she stared up at his darkly brooding face, summoning up all her courage to break the spell he'd woven around her. 'You're asking too much of me!'

'Rules? Whose rules, hmm? I don't remember being a party to any rules.'

Beneath his glowering regard Aphra could feel her heart racing, recognised with a feeling of desolation that she was torn between a powerful physical need and a fastidious mental disinclination to become merely the means of satisfying Luc's sexual appetite.

'You're no shy virgin, little Annie Glover, however much you'd like me to believe that. Your zeal for championing lost lambs may have changed into one for fighting lost causes, but your days of innocence are far behind you.'

Bitterness lodged in his voice as he stared down into her flushed face, his gaze knowing. 'Neither do you find me physically repulsive. Do you think I'm so inexperienced that I can't read the message in your enlarged pupils or the flush in your cheeks?' He gave a soft laugh. 'So give me one good reason why we shouldn't become lovers.'

'Because I don't love you!'

His contemptuous tone had sparked her anger, releasing her from his spell, as to her utter chagrin she felt her cheeks grow even hotter. Oh, dear heavens! No shy virgin indeed! If he only knew!

The rush of fury which assailed her gave her the strength to push Luc away from her. Scrambling to her feet, she turned her back on him, her blonde hair, released from its confining band, swinging around her face as she restored her dishevelled clothes to some semblance of decency.

As if to order, the cicadas resumed their rhythmic cadence, like an orchestra signalling the end of an act in a play. So why did she feel so restless? Why was her pulse still thumping away as if she'd run a marathon?

'What's love got to do with enjoying an intimate relationship?'

Scarcely knowing what she was doing, Aphra spun round to face Luc as he spoke. He'd risen lazily to his feet as she'd fought for control over the wild excitement which seemed to have possessed her usually rational mind.

'Obviously nothing as far as you're concerned!' she retorted acidly. 'And another thing,' she flashed at him, eyeing him closely as he leant silently against one of the pine trees, his expression unreadable, his lips pursed soundlessly. 'You can stop calling me Annie Glover. That was never my name.'

He shrugged. 'It suited your purpose at the time, just like becoming Aphra Benchard suits it now. What I'm suggesting is that we make the latter situation a permanent arrangement.'

'You mean not get divorced after enough time has passed to prevent awkward questions being asked?' Aphra gasped, the sheer audacity of the suggestion taking her breath away. 'But . . . why? What would be the point of it?'

Luc made an impatient gesture with his shoulders. 'Why not? The more I think about it, the more sensible such a course of action seems. Neither of us has made a success of emotional commitments to date, we share the same sentiment about Fairmead, and whatever our views about each other's moral behaviour we don't find each other physically repulsive.' He paused as if waiting for a comment from her, but when she remained silent he continued briskly. 'Financially it makes sense. Even after inheritance tax is paid I shall have ample income to support a wife and family. Believe me, Aphra, you could do a lot worse materially.'

'Not with the kind of divorce settlement I had in mind,' she lied recklessly, horrified that he should appeal to what he saw as her mercenary instincts.

Slowly he shook his head, dark eyes gleaming as they scanned her outraged face. 'Don't count on it, darling. I've been doing my sums very thoroughly and, believe me, your best interests lie in turning this charade into reality.'

Slowly, disbelievingly, Aphra shook her head. 'How long have you been toying with this idea, Luc?' she asked quietly, aware that her heart was pounding uncomfortably.

'Since you agreed to become my obligatory bride,' he admitted coolly.

'But you didn't think it necessary to inform me about your change of heart before the ceremony?' Her voice rose querulously. 'You're the most arrogant—'

'Intelligent,' he corrected her quickly, a sparkle of amusement briefly transforming his stern face. 'I decided you'd probably be more amenable to the suggestion after the wedding, especially when I could put my argument to you in such an isolated, romantic setting.'

'So coming here wasn't just to put Leonard off the scent of our deception,' she said dully.

Luc smiled grimly. 'That was certainly one of its purposes, but not the only one, no,' he admitted. His gaze narrowed and his dark eyes arrowed in on her troubled expression. 'Think about it. You could do a lot worse for yourself in the long term, little Annie Glover.'

And a lot better! she thought hysterically. Somewhere in the world there must be a man who would love her as much as Peter had professed to. A man who would want to marry her because he cared for her and wanted to share his life with her. A man whom she could love as much as she loved Luc, but who would return her love...

She swallowed painfully as the truth struck her. As much as she loved Luc...

'You brought me to Corsica to seduce me,' she said flatly.

'There's something wrong in a man attempting to seduce his wife?'

Not if he loves her, she screamed silently as she sought to find a less betraying answer. 'Yes! If it wasn't part of the premarital agreement.' Bravely she forced herself to meet his eyes.

'Even if we'd drawn up and signed an agreement a clause of non-consummation would have had no legal standing. I'll take nothing from you which isn't freely given,' he responded curtly. 'But I would remind you of one thing: the reason Grand-mère included that troublesome clause in her will was because she wanted to be sure her great-grandchildren and their children would keep her genes alive at Fairmead. She wanted her Corsican blood to be perpetuated through me, her only survivor.'

'What are you saying?' Aphra whispered, spasms of alarm flaring within her. But she already knew. The ominous words 'support a wife and family' had been buzzing around in her subconscious mind ever since he'd uttered them.

Luc shrugged again. 'Nothing extraordinary. Whatever your motives, the fact is that you were a friend and companion to my grandmother when she needed one, and I believe she would have approved of our marriage.

'The best possible way of fulfilling the spirit of Amélie's wishes and thwarting Leonard's destructive plans is for you and me to make certain that we provide the great-grandchildren which Amélie so dearly wanted.'

CHAPTER EIGHT

SHOCK kept Aphra momentarily speechless, then she was struggling to find the words to condemn his suggestion.

'I was ready to give a couple of years of my life to right what was a terrible wrong,' she cried desperately. 'But what you suggest is monstrous—'

'Sell!' Luc interposed roughly. 'You were prepared to *sell* a couple of years of your life. All I'm asking you to do is extend that period. I promise you you'll be well rewarded socially and financially, and if we are blessed with a child then you'll have the satisfaction of knowing that Amélie will be resting peacefully wherever she is.'

'You can't blackmail me with sentiment!' Aphra cried desperately. 'There's no way I'd consider bearing the child of a man I didn't love and admire, or one who didn't return those feelings.'

'Then you could be making a bad mistake,' Luc returned coolly. 'Many people believe that a civilised arranged marriage forms a far better environment for the health and well-being of the participants, as well as the children of the union, than one confused by such metaphysical concepts as love.' He paused and allowed his gaze to drift over her impersonally. 'Of course, physical compatibility is an added bonus for both partners, and frankly I don't think we would experience any problems in that area, do you?'

'Let go of me!' Vainly she tried to elude his steady grip, bewildered by his callous dismissal of the embryonic emotion which was already beginning to torture her with its persistence. 'I don't want to discuss this.'

'Tough! Because I do,' he persisted hardily. Beneath his cynical regard Aphra felt her senses spinning. Pushing her soft hair back from her hot forehead with shaking fingers, she was aware of some dark force in Luc's eyes making it impossible for her to move away, although he no longer held her captive with his hands.

'You must know how I feel about you,' she protested, her voice little more than a whisper, her nervous system tingling in response to the sensual undertones of the question.

'You despise me. Yes, you've made that quite clear.' His short laugh dismissed her protest with scant regard. 'But don't fool yourself, Aphra. Liking has nothing to do with making love. Physical attraction is a chemical reaction which doesn't make moral judgements. All you need is the desire.' Dark eyes drifted over her dishevelled appearance. 'And, despite your protestations, I think you do desire me. Because when I touch you I feel your response. When I put my hand on your breast, I feel your flesh leap to my caress—'

'No...' Her protest was almost a moan as she felt a rising tide of warmth sweep through her body.

'Oh, yes, my sweet,' he continued softly, his eyes raking perceptively over her flushed face. 'You weren't born for a life of celibacy and denial. You know that as well as I do.' Raising a hand, he traced the line of her cheek while she stood motionless, transfixed by the spell he was weaving around her.

'Last night,' she began breathlessly, 'you said—'

'Last night we were both tired and you were in no mood to admit the truth.' His voice was husky, a murmur against her skin as he lowered his mouth to the softness of her cheek, bestowing on it the lightest of caresses. 'You may hate yourself for it, Aphra, but the fact is, you want to make love with me as much as I want to with you.'

She wanted to deny it, but the damp warmth of his lips against her face was a distraction which numbed her mind, depriving her of the power of speech, so she could only utter a small moan as his mouth traced a line of tiny kisses down to the tender hollow at her throat.

Her body taughtened as mortification filled her. How was it possible for her to respond to Luc's mindless expertise, when she knew that his only purpose was to quench the physical need which was racking him, that it was still Kathryn Bellini whom he loved?

Vividly she recalled his bitter words after their wedding reception when he'd referred with such longing to his lost love. 'Do you find a substitute lover and close your eyes when you kiss...?' he had asked her. She shivered, remembering how he had illustrated his meaning then, punishing her for the crime of not being the right bride, for not being Kathryn.

Now it was different. All during the previous day she'd felt the tension building between them. Like a powerful tide it had flowed, entrapping her, despite the efforts she had made to repel it. Somehow in the interim years between their meetings, her admiration and hero-worship of Luc had become a more durable emotion. With a sinking heart she could no longer deny to herself that she loved him.

Taking her silence for acquiescence, a sigh of pleasure slid out from between Luc's barely parted lips. Then his arms had encompassed her, pulling her hard against his taut body as, fiercely demanding, his mouth possessed hers.

There was power and passion in his kiss—and something else, akin to anger, she realised despairingly. It wasn't the first time Luc had kissed her with such latent carnality. Too aware of the hard masculinity of his body imprinting its warmth on her yielding softness, she made no attempt to fight him, surrendering to the assault on her senses with a feeling of inevitability. At that moment, there was nothing, no one else in the world but Luc.

His fingers climbed her back with swift and silent purpose, undoing the catch of her bra with the skill of an expert, before gently seeking to cup the fullness he had released, sighing with enjoyment as her warm flesh spilled into the bowl of his hand and he felt the rigid pressure of her nipple taut against the gentle caress of his thumb.

Then, before she'd realised his intention, he pushed aside the soft cotton of her top which had afforded her some modesty, and buried his face between her uncovered breasts.

A small sob of pleasurable anguish issued from Aphra's throat as her senses reacted to the erotic mixture of warm air and Luc's heated skin against her naked flesh. Her hands clinging to his shoulders as she leant away from him, she tipped her head backwards, her hair swinging in disarray as she offered herself to his gratification.

Nothing she'd read or seen or experienced had prepared her for the frightening tumult of her own arousal—or warned her about the yawning ache which was spreading inexorably through her body as, with a sigh, she raised her hands from the muscular firmness of Luc's arms and shoulders to caress the soft dark hair of his head.

He had been right. To her shame she admitted it. Even knowing that he was embittered by Kathryn's defection, that his heart was not on offer and that all he was seeking was temporary satisfaction for his own frustrated hunger, she wanted him, as she had never wanted any other man in her life.

For a timeless moment Luc became her whole universe; her senses filled with his touch, his scent, the hunting power of his strong masculine body as he eased her down once more on the bed of pine needles at their feet, but this time with a gentleness which drained away any last remnants of resistance she might have harboured. But there had been none.

He could take her here, in the forest, consummate their marriage in this magic place of warmth and sweetness to the accompaniment provided by the invisible orchestra of cicadas, and she would be his willing partner—not only for this fevered moment, but, as he had suggested, for the rest of her life.

Seconds later, the soft tinkle of bells penetrated her mind, accompanied by a sound which seemed vaguely familiar.

'Luc—someone's coming!' She struggled beneath him, sudden panic overwhelming her. Only when she felt Luc reluctantly ease his body away from hers and felt him cover her breasts with her top did she start to relax.

'It must be some other hikers, or people from the village.' Her voice was soft and shaky as she made an effort to calm her heated senses. How humiliating if someone had discovered them locked in each other's arms—or worse! She felt a blush consume her whole body as she considered what sight might have met their eyes in another few minutes.

'Sheep,' Luc vouchsafed succinctly, his face dark with frustration, his jaw tight with annoyance. 'It's just a herd of itinerant sheep which has strayed from its usual pasture. For pity's sake...' He emitted an exasperated sigh. 'It must be my destiny to have my plans for amorous adventures thwarted by sheep! Just what is it with you and sheep, Aphra?'

'Perhaps they're repaying a debt,' she offered, pulling herself upright as the sensual spell which Luc had woven around her shattered. She was trembling, her breathing fast and shallow, her body experiencing an almost unbearable emptiness that had nothing to do with lack of food.

She tried to swallow, but her mouth was too dry. 'They probably share a group memory,' she forced herself to continue, taking an odd comfort in the fact that, if appearances went for anything, Luc seemed to be feeling worse than she did. Her eyes strayed to where he was pushing his T-shirt back into the waistband of his jeans, before rising quickly to dwell on his glowering face.

'I saved one of their clan from a fate worse than death and now they're repaying the favour.' She scrambled to her feet, arranging her clothes with fingers which were unsteady. Saved by the bell, she thought hysterically, and bit her lip to avoid laughing aloud.

Luc's dark eyes searched her flushed face. 'There's no need to be scared. They may look a bit strange to your English eyes, but they won't hurt you.'

'Probably not,' she returned coolly, feeling her pulse regaining its normal tranquil rhythm as she experienced a wave of deep gratitude that her mindless surrender had been aborted. 'But where there's sheep there may be a shepherd, and, according to you, *they* can be quite dangerous when aroused!'

'It wasn't the shepherd I had in mind to arouse,' Luc returned equably. 'Besides, according to legend, they only overreact when their own womenfolk are compromised. Doubtless, blue-eyed blondes of doubtful heritage are free to gambol where and with whom they please. But you're quite right. Like you, I prefer to perform without an audience. I think we could discuss our plans for the future more profitably back home.'

Home. The word made her shiver as she followed Luc out of the forest's shade. It suggested
so much that she wanted and had never really enjoyed—family, cosiness, people liking and loving
each other, working for a common purpose,
children . . .

Doggedly she fell into step behind him as he
stepped out into the heat of the late afternoon. Luc
wanted none of those long-term pleasures. He
wanted a compliant woman in his bed, a hostess at
his table and a competent mother for his heirs.
Kathryn Bellini had a lot to answer for, she decided
sadly. Whatever had happened between the two of
them had left Luc bereft of affection and
tenderness.

The slowly ascending track was hard and stony,
traversed now and again by slowly moving columns
of large ants. The pungent scent of the maquis hung
on the still air as Aphra drank in the beauty of their
surroundings. On one side the granite cliffs towered
towards the cloudless sky, their outlines sculptured
by nature into weird and wonderful shapes.

Tortured creatures with grotesque faces and mal-
formed bodies appeared to cling to outcrops of
rock, whilst soaring pillars of stone stood starkly
beautiful like cloisters of some medieval cathedral,
reaching upwards from the dark carpet of maquis
clinging to their bases.

On the other side, the cliff extended several
metres before tumbling in layers towards the distant
sea. Aphra paused, enjoying the brief respite to rest
her weary legs, aware of the heartbeat of nature as
the crickets thrummed incessantly and the wild bees

murmured in seeming contentment as they gorged themselves on the abundant flowering shrubs which covered the terrain.

'Is the going too tough for you?'

Luc must have sensed that she was no longer close behind him for he turned to confront her labouring figure.

'No!' Quickly she denied her tiredness, believing she glimpsed a gleam of triumph in his darkly perceptive eyes. Is that what he wanted? To make her life difficult? To punish her for not being Kathryn? Or was weariness making her psychotic? She sighed, knowing herself trapped, almost hypnotised by the magic of her surroundings. 'I paused for a moment to admire the scenery.'

'Magnificent, isn't it?' He spoke softly. 'The erosion of the rocks is due to their unique crystal structure. They even change colour with the time of day. The deep ochre you're admiring now will turn to rose by the time the sun begins to set—although by then we will be well on our way back. If you were here when the sun sank behind the horizon they would appear purple.'

'How very theatrical.' She stole a glance at Luc's face, surprised at the intensity of his expression, as if he, too, felt the mysticism of their surroundings. 'Have you been here at sunset?'

'When I was much younger.' He fell into step beside her, treading on the rougher ground beside the path. 'Grand-mère encouraged me to make the journey, but despite my pleas she would never come back with me.'

He shrugged. 'Perhaps as she grew older she felt she'd betrayed her family; perhaps she was afraid of vengeance even then. Perhaps she simply felt that she had closed a door and that there was no point in reopening it. In retrospect she made the right decision. By the time I began trying to trace my roots, they'd disintegrated. The family had disappeared, the older ones dead, the younger ones gone to the mainland in search of a more secure future.'

'So there was nothing here for you.' Aphra sensed his disappointment, the keenness of the frustration he must have felt, and impulsively touched his arm in sympathy.

'Only the island. Only La Corse herself.' To Aphra's surprise he took her hand, holding it loosely in his own. 'Can you understand that, Aphra? Can you comprehend how it's possible to fall in love with a place, to be bewitched by its ghosts, so that every time you walk on its soil you feel as if you are returning to a long-forsaken and dearly loved home?'

'I understand.' Her voice was little more than a whisper as she turned her head to regard his set profile. Didn't he realise that was how *she* felt about Fairmead? And how she was beginning to feel about this place too? Despite the heat of the afternoon she shivered. 'The atmosphere of some places seems to cast a spell, so that their image lingers in your mind long after you've left their boundaries.'

'And demands that you return.' Luc nodded as his fingers entwined with hers. 'And each time you do you believe you'll be able to break the spell, to get possession of your senses back again, but you never can because, each time, you discover some new facet, some new, enchanting secret that binds you ever closer. It's said that to love passionately there always needs to be something left to discover. Perhaps it's because Corsica yields her innermost secrets so reluctantly that she remains irresistible to me.'

He'd said Corsica, but did he mean Kathryn? A growing ache in the region of her heart told Aphra that it was the latter who dominated his thoughts. If she accepted Luc's suggestion to honour the spirit of their marriage then she would have to come to terms with the fact that she would only ever be second best as far as he was concerned.

Yet, two hours later when, in the shadow of the cottage, Luc stopped to confront her, drawing her fully into his arms, she was ready for him, her lips parting beneath the gentle pressure of his tongue, accepting its intimate caress, her soft body yielding to discover and encourage the hardness of his desire.

A treacherous rush of excitement flooded her senses as she responded to the tremor which shuddered through his strong body when Luc recognised her total surrender to sensual pleasure. Then one of his hands was lacing itself through her soft hair, supporting her head, as his mouth trailed a line of soft kisses down her neck, and she heard him groan as his soft lips touched the lightly scented skin which swelled above the minimal control of her summer bra.

Sensation ran like mercury through her nervous system as she clung to his strong shoulders, arching her back in an instinctive gesture of welcome as her whole system responded to a savage hunger she was experiencing for the first time in her life. Her response in the pine woods had been but a mere overture to the crescendo of feeling which now surged through her body.

'You do want me, my Aphrodite.' His voice was husky and edged with something like pain. 'If you have any honour in you, you can't deny it.'

Aphra sighed as instinctively her hands moved possessively upwards, her fingers seeking the strong column of his neck before threading through the dark crispness of his thick hair, even while her mind flinched away from the cruel reference to her honour.

'Say it! Admit that you want this as much as I do!' he instructed her harshly. 'For pity's sake, be honest with me, Aphra, before it's too late.'

'And if I don't admit it, what then?' Unaware of whether the question was a last-minute attempt to salvage her pride or a deeply ingrained desire to discover if the hero of her youthful dreams still existed, she anxiously scanned Luc's intent face, while her heart thudded with painful intensity against her ribcage.

'I shall accept your decision, of course,' he returned savagely. 'But you'll spend the night here alone and tomorrow we'll leave for Leamarsh.' He paused, the planes of his face taut as he pushed her from his embrace. 'So? The decision's yours.'

'I—I . . .' She knew she was going to surrender herself to him, assuage not only *his* desire but the torment which was raging inside her own virginal body, and she could only pray that her inexperience would not spoil their mutual pleasure.

Even in the heat of that knowledge she realised she could preserve an atom of her pride. He need never know that her sole motivation was her love for him.

'But I don't want to go back yet,' she protested, forcing her soft mouth into a pout. 'Besides, think how bad it would look from Leonard's point of view. I thought it was for his benefit that we came here in the first place.'

Luc's mouth curved into a hard, glittering smile of triumph as he ignored her querulous comment. 'Is that your way of saying yes?'

She nodded.

'Say it, Aphra!' His hand slid down her arm, his fingers tightening round her wrist. 'I don't want there to be any misunderstanding about what's happening here. If you say yes now, then our marriage ceases to be platonic. Is that what you want?'

'I want...' Her voice faltered and she scanned his dark face, seeking some sign of affection but seeing only the hard glitter of arousal which lent his features a feral splendour. She paused, unable to tell him how deep were her emotional needs. 'Yes,' she said simply. 'That's what I want.'

The next moment she was swept off her feet as Luc swung her into his arms. Clasping her hard against his chest, he paused only for a moment to open the heavy door of the cottage, before kicking it closed behind them and carrying her into the dark interior of the bedroom.

Setting her on her feet, deftly he began to undress her with practised fingers, his gentle hands loosening the fastening of her jeans and stripping them off. She lifted her arms to assist him as he seized the bottom of her T-shirt and pulled it efficiently over her lowered head. The simple cotton bra which nestled beneath it posed no problem to his expertise, and gathering her revealed softness into his arms, his voice thick and inarticulate, he muttered something unintelligible against her burning skin.

Perhaps it was Kathryn's name, perhaps it was some epithet of desire—Aphra didn't know. She only knew that his mouth was warm and damp against the tumescent peaks of her breasts, causing her to whimper in delight as she pressed herself unashamedly against him.

Until now she'd never dared admit how much she'd longed for this moment, never guessed how easily her body could be roused to such a pitch of ecstasy, so that she felt achingly empty as she anticipated Luc's invasion.

'Luc, wait—stop!' Urgently she strained away from him, her hands rising to push against his shoulders. 'This isn't fair...' Unwillingly he raised his head to meet her troubled gaze, the pupils of his eyes enormous in the filtered light which touched the bed with golden fingers, his expression dazed.

Instantly she realised he thought she'd changed her mind. Moving quickly to reassure him, her hands rose to the buttons of his shirt. 'I want to touch you too—all of you.'

'Oh, dear God!' It was a devout cry of relief as he stepped back, tearing his shirt from his own back, before loosening the belt at his waist. In moments he was naked, as beautiful as she had always known he would be. Taut and sculptured, his broad shoulders were smoothly muscled as he reached for her, lifting her once more in his arms, carrying her to the bed, kneeling over her to remove the last barrier which separated them.

He loved her with his hands and his mouth with a tenderness and expertise which could have fooled her into believing that he loved her with his heart and his soul if she hadn't known better, and she responded to his touch, moving against him in tune with her own internal rhythm as she caressed the hard curves of his body, until she was trembling with anticipation and a yawning hunger that craved the final fulfilment of total possession.

She was whimpering with pleasure, reaching to guide him to herself, when he whispered, 'Just a moment...'

She moaned softly in frustration as he turned away, then he was back beside her, slipping a pillow beneath her hips, poising himself above her as she imprisoned him by sliding her slender legs to entrap him, raising her arms to embrace his shoulders, and he entered her easily, filling the aching void within her, so that she gasped with longing, wanting to be one with him, wanting more than anything in the world for this magic moment never to end.

With the first hard thrust of Luc's body, she cried out, her head twisting on the pillow, her eyes closed, her every sense alive to his presence—to his face buried against her throat, to his teeth gently nipping at her skin, to his hair, soft yet crisp, against her neck.

As the tension mounted inside her she was answering Luc's passion with heated abandon, responding like a flame nourished by fuel. Then, when she thought that there was nothing left to experience, that she had climbed the summit of desire, a feeling of utter ecstasy encapsulated her, like a spontaneous explosion of joy, spreading through every cell of her body. Almost instantly, Luc shuddered violently against her and then lay still.

Long after Luc's soft, steady breathing announced that he had drifted into sleep, Aphra lay still, trying to come to terms with her feelings. Was it possible that ever since she had first known him she had unconsciously anticipated this moment of fulfilment?

It was something she was reluctant to admit to herself, but how else could she explain the flood of emotion which had thrilled through her whole being, lifting her to another plane of sensation?

In the dusk she sighed softly, admitting that Luc was right. They shared a common cause and a physical compatibility. Would those two things provide a strong enough foundation on which to build a life together—a life which would justify her bearing his child?

CHAPTER NINE

LUC was still asleep when Aphra awakened the following morning. Raising herself on one arm, she bent over him, drinking in the sight of his face—the dark stubble on his firm jaw, the thick lashes fanned against his cheekbone, the tousled wealth of jet hair buried in the white pillow.

Her gaze wandered down his body, naked above the swirl of duvet which covered his loins, pausing to appraise a thick serrated scar which traced an uneven path for about ten centimetres across his ribcage.

It looked as if it had been inflicted recently. During his absence in South America? Frustration nagged at her as she realised how little she knew about his life over the past few years.

Perhaps in the coming days he would fill in some of the gaps so that they would become less of emotional strangers. She could only hope so. At the same time she would have to put him right about her own past, she acknowledged unwillingly.

It wasn't something she was looking forward to doing, chiefly because it would bring her motives for agreeing to marry him into a sharper focus than she would have wished. But if their union was to have any chance of succeeding it could not be based on a platform of lies and half-truths. Particularly if they were going to have a family.

Carefully she bent over him, savouring the warm, spicy scent of his skin as she brushed her lips against his shoulder in a butterfly kiss. The previous night had been one of sensual pleasure interspersed with long periods of sleep and refreshing glasses of cool wine.

When neither of them had shown any inclination to get dressed and wander down to the village for an evening meal Luc had even provided a late-night snack of smoked salmon sandwiches. Food for seduction, she'd thought wryly, reluctantly admiring the efficient way in which he had planned to lay siege to her.

Seconds later she was in the bathroom refreshing herself beneath the shower before dressing in a flared denim skirt topped with a sleeveless cotton blouse tied at the waist. Miraculously her feet showed no signs of damage from yesterday's long walk, she noticed complacently, sliding them into comfortable wedge-heeled sandals. Hopefully Luc's plans for today would be less strenuous—or at least, she amended silently, less tiring for her legs!

She smoothed a high-factor sun-protection cream into the delicate skin of her face, before fixing her hair into a neat plait.

This morning *she* would prepare breakfast. A quick search through the cupboards in the large sitting room revealed a packet of filter coffee together with an electric percolator, plus an assortment of crockery and cutlery.

Another cupboard proved to house a small refrigerator stocked with a minimum of basics in-

cluding soft drinks, butter and a selection of
confitures.

Luc was still asleep when she peeped round the
bedroom door. No need to wake him. The stroll to
the village and back would take less than thirty
minutes, she calculated, and if he did awaken and
miss her he'd guess where she'd gone. Collecting
her handbag from the bedside table, she closed the
door quietly behind her as she left.

Even at eight in the morning the sun bathed her
skin with its warmth. The air was still, laced with
the heady perfume of the maquis, as she took the
winding path which would lead to the centre of the
village.

She walked slowly, her inner body still joyfully
aware of Luc's penetration, as she allowed her
senses to absorb the essence of this alien land, and
her thoughts wandered back to Amélie. What would
Luc's grandmother think if she could see her now?

She was on her way back with a baguette and
four fragrant croissants when she was forced to
move sharply to the side of the path to allow a small
red Renault to overtake her in a cloud of dust.

Whoever was driving it was obviously in a hurry,
and not an over-considerate driver either, she decided ruefully, pausing to brush some dirt and grit
away from her clothes.

Minutes later, as she turned the bend in the road,
she saw to her surprise that the car had pulled in
outside Amélie's cottage. Curious, she began to
walk faster. Who on earth could be paying a call
this early in the morning?

Using the spare key which she'd taken from its place beside the front door, she fumbled impatiently at the lock before bursting into the vestibule, then froze to the spot as a woman's voice, soft and breathless, filtered through the opening of the door in front of her.

'Once I discovered what had happened to you in Venezuela, I had to find you and let you know how sorry I am about the way we parted.'

'Happened to me?' Luc's voice was softly mocking, with the echo of pain that she had come to recognise. 'A great many things happened to me in Venezuela. Which one in particular has incited your contrition, Kathryn?'

Kathryn! It was as if a block of ice had suddenly surrounded Aphra's heart. Rooted to the ground in shock, she waited to hear Kathryn's reply.

'Oh, don't pretend, Luc!' Kathryn chided. 'Your story's just made front-page news in the States. BRITISH VISITOR TO SOUTH AMERICA IN KIDNAP ORDEAL. COMPANY DIRECTOR MISTAKEN FOR US SENATOR. PROLONGED ORDEAL OF MISSING TOURIST. I only found out yesterday when one of my friends in the USA phoned me where I was staying in Nice and told me the full story.'

Oh, dear God! Feeling a wave of faintness surge through her body, Aphra leant for support against the wall of the lobby. Kathryn Bellini here, in Corsica, and obviously bent on a reconciliation with Luc. It was the stuff of nightmares.

And what was this about a kidnap? Her mind spun as she tried to make sense of what she'd overheard. Was it possible that Luc had not, after all, been guilty of deliberately neglecting his grand-mother, but had been physically deprived of the opportunity to keep in touch? It was a chilling thought and one she was finding hard to assimilate as Luc's voice reached her ears once more.

'How did you find me?'

'I phoned your home in England yesterday morning as soon as I heard, and spoke to some caretaker person who told me your grandmother had died recently and that you'd just got married and were in Corsica on your honeymoon.'

She gave a soft laugh. 'Of course, I realised im-mediately you'd only married to keep your title to your grandmother's old house and the whole set-up was nothing but a sham. And where else in Corsica would you have hidden your convenient bride but in this dump? Do you think I've for-gotten that time you brought me here and how passionate about the place you were?' She sighed languidly. 'But then you're a very passionate man, Luc. I haven't forgotten that either. That's why I'm here. Oh, darling, you can't imagine how much I've missed you!'

The soft feminine voice faltered as Aphra stood frozen, motionless, knowing that she shouldn't be eavesdropping. She should either enter the room or return to the village, but neither option would satisfy the painful curiosity which was holding her heart in an icy grip.

Silently, and with a hand which trembled, she pushed the door to the sitting room slightly ajar, so that she could peer through the narrow opening.

Kathryn and Luc were standing at the far side of the table, Luc stripped to the waist, his denim jeans, unbelted, riding low on his hips, his hair still tousled from sleep, as if he had just got out of bed—which he probably had.

Kathryn was immaculate in a sleeveless, close-fitting scarlet cotton knit sheath-dress, her dark chestnut hair cut in a short, silky bob which set off the perfection of her small, chiselled features.

Aphra had expected her to be tall and willowy, but she looked tiny against Luc's muscled stature. Of course—she readjusted her thoughts—it was the camera to which Kathryn appealed, not the catwalk. A spasm of pain made her feel sick and empty.

Luc had been dreadfully hurt and his pride was making him slow in yielding to Kathryn's present seduction, but yield he would, she was certain. How could any man who had once loved the exquisite woman whose hand now stroked his bare arm be expected to resist her when she had so obviously come to make amends?

'You want us to be lovers again? To take up our lives as if nothing had happened?' The husky warmth of Luc's deep tones, an echo from the previous night, made Aphra wince in painful anguish as Kathryn, lifting her beautiful profile, her lips parted in open invitation, pressed herself against his body.

'Of course,' she purred. 'It's what you want too, my love.'

'And what about your husband?' Luc smiled down at her indulgently. 'How will *he* fit into this new arrangement?'

'Oh, him!' A shrug dismissed Luc's objection. 'Felipe was a bad mistake. He just happened to be around when I thought you'd deserted me. He was good-looking and persuasive, so I accepted his proposal, but I never loved him.'

'Are you telling me your marriage hasn't worked out?' Luc stared down into Kathryn's lovely face as Aphra's fingernails dug deeply into the palms of her hands.

She shrugged again. 'How could it when you were the only man I ever loved?' Looping her arms around Luc's neck, she pulled his face down towards her own, smiling into his dark eyes. 'And I know you still love me.' Tilting her head, she offered her mouth for his kiss, confidence in every line of her curvaceous form, as Aphra bit her lips to silence the moan of pain which rose to them.

'And the fact that I have a wife doesn't bother you?' Luc murmured, lifting one hand to trap her beautifully moulded chin.

'Why should it?' Kathryn was cruelly dismissive. 'Some little nobody who happened to be in the right place at the right time and acted as a stand-in for me? I'm sure you've already made plans to pay her off. Bring them forward a little—offer her more!'

As if in a trance, Aphra watched as Luc's eyes travelled slowly over Kathryn's eager face and lissom body. 'You still believe there's a future for you and me together—after everything that's happened?' he asked softly.

'Yes, of course. Don't tease me, Luc!' Eagerly she reached out to him. 'You can't blame me for what happened. You'd been like a bear with a sore

head for days. I couldn't do anything right for you,
and then when you wouldn't come with me to that
reception and I thought you'd left me in the lurch
the next day—well, I was understandably furious!
But that's all in the past—'

'But my marriage is very much in the present,
Kathryn.' The lines of Luc's face were tightly drawn
as he seized her wrists, pulling them away from his
body. 'Aphra is my legal wife and not so easily dis-
posed of.'

His legal wife. Aphra's eyes filled with tears of
pain and humiliation. Yet what had she expected
to hear—that he loved her? There was no comfort
in his bleak assertion. All he was doing was punishing Kathryn, dragging out the time, before he
succumbed to her blatant charms. La Bella Bellini
had hurt him badly, but he would forgive her; every
aching cell in Aphra's body sensed his imminent
capitulation as Kathryn drew in her breath in a deep
sob.

'Luc, darling, don't be difficult!' Kathryn's voice
trembled dramatically. 'You can't turn your back
on me; you can't! You know you love me. You
always have...'

'But now I have other obligations,' Luc told her
harshly. 'It's about time you realised that not all
of us are slaves to our hormones. Some of us recognise there are more important responsibilities in
life—'

'Yes, yes! Do you think I don't know that?'
Frantically, Kathryn clutched at his arms, a thread
of desperation harshening her voice. 'That's why
I'm here, why it was so important to see you

without delay. I didn't want to break it to you like this, but there's something you've got to know.'

'Go on,' Luc directed harshly.

She caught her breath in a sob. 'In Venezuela, when you didn't come to pick me up at the hotel, I was distraught. I began to believe that you didn't love me after all. So I went back to the States, hoping you would follow, but of course you didn't and then—then...' She paused dramatically. 'Then a few weeks later I discovered I was pregnant!

'Can you imagine how I felt? I was at my wits' end. You hadn't made any attempt to get in touch with me and by then I'd met Felipe and he was begging me to marry him. It seemed the easiest way out so I said yes. I thought, when the baby was born, I could persuade Felipe that it was premature, that he was the father.' She paused to rub the back of one hand beneath her eyes.

A suffocating tension tightened in Aphra's throat as, transfixed, she watched a wave of shock turn Luc's features to stone.

'He—he didn't believe me, Luc. He insisted on blood and DNA tests,' Kathryn persevered. 'He was an absolute *brute*! When he got the results, he threw me out. Told me to go to the father of my child.' There were tears running down her cheeks. 'That's why I'm here, Luc. Punish me if you must, but don't take it out on our baby. Don't turn your back on your son!'

As Kathryn flung herself against Luc and as he opened his arms to support her, Aphra moved blindly away from the door. It was the final death blow to the tiny flame of hope burning deep in her heart that, given time, she and Luc might enjoy a companionable future.

His son! Kathryn had borne Luc a son, the first great-grandchild which Amélie had longed to see—a little boy who would inherit the beauty and tradition of Fairmead, with his mother and father there at his side.

Tortured by anguish, she let the broken baguette fall from her nerveless fingers to find a resting place on the narrow table beneath the row of coat hooks, followed by the bag of croissants. There was nothing left for her here. Kathryn and Luc needed time together to celebrate their reunion, and for Luc to rejoice in his new role of a father.

Stumbling from the cottage, she closed the front door behind her, poignantly aware that Luc and Kathryn were too engaged with each other to hear the slight sound it made.

Then she was running, taking the road to the village, her one thought to find sanctuary somewhere, anywhere where she could be alone and attempt to come to terms with her grief, and make plans for the future.

Breath sawing in her chest, calves aching from the spurt of speed she'd dredged up to hasten her flight, she slowed to a jog before reaching the centre of the small community. She desperately needed somewhere where she could sit down to evaluate what she had overheard and to decide what to do for the best.

On the way to the baker's she had passed the inn—probably the same one where Luc's grandfather had been compromised by Amélie, she thought numbly. Where better to take refuge to consider where her own future now lay?

As she approached its forecourt she was aware of the scent of coffee and newly baked bread emanating from within its time-weathered walls, and heard the slight murmur of conversation.

Wearily she sank down on one of the old wooden benches fixed against the wall, and, leaning forward, rested her elbows on the trestle-table in front of her. Eyes narrowed against the brightness of the morning sun, she stared unseeingly across the countryside towards where the sky and sea met in an indiscernible line of haze.

A baby. Kathryn had had a baby and Luc was the father. The reality scorched into her heart like a branding-iron. She had no one to blame but herself for the pain, but that realisation brought her no comfort. Luc had never lied to her, never pretended to care for her as a person. Last night, she'd fooled herself into believing that the two of them might be able to find some compensation in their arranged marriage after all.

She'd been wrong. What they'd shared last night hadn't been a platform on which a greater understanding and tolerance could be built. It had been an explosion of ecstasy as exquisite and ephemeral as a sandcastle which collapses at the first surge of the incoming tide. Kathryn's reappearance had provided the destructive power necessary to crush her embryonic dreams.

Beneath the surface of her pain lingered the question of Luc's abduction, and a growing feeling of guilt as she recollected the way she'd greeted him on his return to Fairmead. Little wonder that he held her in such low esteem!

She'd acted as his judge and his jury and found him guilty of negligence without having asked for or waited for one word of explanation. She shivered, remembering the vicious cicatrix which had crossed his ribs. Dear heavens! No wonder he had reacted to her presence in Amélie's home with such animosity. The least she could do now was to behave with some degree of dignity.

'*Madame?*' Aphra's thoughts were interrupted by the appearance of a middle-aged woman from the interior of the building. '*Vous desirez le petit déjeuner?*'

'*Un café au lait, seulement, s'il vous plait.*' Aphra attempted a smile as the woman nodded. Any food would have stuck in her throat. Even coffee was going to be difficult to swallow past the lump which nervous tension had caused to constrict her gullet.

When the coffee came it was served in a bowl, which meant she had to use both hands to raise it to her mouth. It was hot and stimulating, a welcome antidote to the shock which had stunned her mental processes.

One thing was clear. She couldn't stay in Corsica. Luc and Kathryn had to have time together to seal their reunion both physically and mentally. Her presence on the island, let alone in the same village, would be intolerable and embarrassing both to them and to herself while they worked out plans for their future together.

Aphra sighed. What a mess. Heaven knew what the legal solution would be to Luc's inheritance problem, but whatever it was she would go along with it. At least he wouldn't be required to pay her off! That information would doubtless come as a pleasant surprise to both him and Kathryn. Her mouth twisted wryly. It would be her wedding present to them, when circumstances permitted them to come together as fate had obviously determined they should!

Luc's baby. A needle-sharp pain seared Aphra's heart. Even if it hadn't been obvious that Luc's enchantment with Kathryn had survived the terrible circumstances which had separated them, Luc would never have turned his back on his own child.

Retreat to Fairmead was equally impossible. There was no way she could arrive unexpectedly and alone in Leamarsh without arousing the kind of gossip which could start tongues wagging and destroy Luc's plans for the future.

The solution, then, was obvious. She would fly back to England and head for her parents' apartment in London, leaving the newly reunited lovebirds together in their Corsican nest to make their peace. Fortunately she had her own gold card with her, so arranging a flight wouldn't be difficult, although there might be some delay before she could get a seat.

Now she was thinking positively she began to feel better. Of course she couldn't just disappear without a word. That would put an impossible burden on Luc at a time when he needed to concentrate on his renewed relationship with Kathryn. On the other hand the last thing she wanted was the two of them appearing at her parents' flat until she'd come to terms with the dissolution of her own dreams.

No, when she saw Luc again it would be on her own terms and at a neutral rendezvous nominated by herself. That was easy. Having decided on a plan of action, she tore a page out of the diary she carried around with her and after a few moments' thought wrote a simple message. 'I am returning to the UK to enable you and Kathryn to enjoy the privacy you need. Please ring my solicitor when you go back and he will arrange a meeting between us to discuss future plans.'

She added her solicitor's phone number and signed the note with her initial. All she needed to do now was to arrange for it to be delivered to Amélie's cottage, but not before she'd found a way to get out of the village.

Luck was on her side. Entering the bar, she found the woman who had served her coffee chatting to a couple of young men dressed in traditional hikers' gear. A tentative question about the possibility of hiring a car to take her to Porto brought forth the information that the inn's proprietor was leaving for that destination in a few moments' time to purchase fresh fish from the market and would be delighted to give her a lift in exchange for suitable recompense.

The note, too, would prove no problem. One of the hikers volunteered to drop it in at the cottage on his way past after he and his companion had ordered and eaten their breakfast.

So, after all, the first stage of leaving Luc had been easy. Seated in the front of the van next to the driver, Aphra was grateful for his silence. The pain of leaving the island was nearly as acute as that of leaving Luc. One day she would weep, but for now tears remained an unattainable comfort. Dry-eyed, she watched the passing countryside, drinking in its savage beauty, inhaling the potent scent of the ever present maquis.

Her body ached all over. If she had been superstitious she might have believed that somewhere, somehow Amélie knew of her flight and was using powerful invisible bonds to restrain her. She rubbed her wrists, wondering at the tricks imagination could play.

It wasn't in her nature to cede anything without a fight. Last night she had dreamed, hoped that Luc had felt some kind of affection for her. He had shown a tenderness and consideration beyond the demands of physical satisfaction alone. For those few brief hours she had dared to hope. 'Some of us recognise there are more important responsibilities . . .' he had told Kathryn. The words of an honourable man, but she had never wanted to be his responsibility. How could she have guessed how soon her dreams would be shattered beyond repair?

Porto was already crowded by the time the van pulled up in the connecting road between the coastal route and the town centre, and Aphra alighted, paying and thanking the taciturn driver.

Already plans were forming in her mind. She needed more cash in hand, a change of clothes, toiletries and cosmetics but, above all, transport to the city of Ajaccio. Once there she stood more chance of booking herself into a hotel room if, as she suspected, she might have a few days to wait for a spare seat on a flight.

It was late the same evening when she arrived at her destination, and later still before she found a vacant room in a hotel and flung herself down, fully clothed on the comfortable bed, to find relief for the first time in tears.

Three days later she was back in London, facing a temperature which was discernibly lower. Again fortune had smiled on her, as she'd been able to get a cancelled seat on a charter flight direct to Gatwick.

Pushing open the entrance door to the lobby of the elegant apartment block which contained her London home, she smiled at the hall porter on duty behind the mahogany reception desk.

'Miss Beaumont-Valance!' He rose to his feet, a similar smile of greeting complementing the surprise in his voice. 'I'm afraid we weren't expecting you...'

'No, it was a spur-of-the-moment decision.' She allowed him to relieve her of the leather grip which contained her emergency luggage. How odd it was to hear her maiden name spoken again. But then the porter knew nothing of her ill-fated marriage to Peter or her present traumatic liaison with Luc. To him she was the idle dilletante daughter of very wealthy parents.

'I'll have this brought up to your apartment right away.' He snapped his fingers imperiously for a lesser lackey to carry out his orders. 'And I'll send the housekeeper to you immediately. Is there anything else I can do for you?'

'Let me have the spare key to the apartment.' She smiled again, wryly. 'I left in rather a hurry and I didn't bring it with me. Oh, and Harris, I've been out of the country for a few days; I'd like to catch up on the news. Do you have any back issues of the national press I could look at?'

An hour later, freshly bathed and relaxing on her bed with a glass of wine beside her and a freshly made prawn salad sandwich, she found what she had hoped for.

BUSINESSMAN IN KIDNAP DRAMA ran the headlines, and in smaller type underneath, MISTAKEN IDENTITY LEADS TO PROLONGED JUNGLE ORDEAL FOR BRITISH TOURIST.

CHAPTER TEN

IT WAS all there. Aphra's supposition that the tabloids would have picked up the story from the American press had been fully justified. One of the popular dailies had even devoted a double-page spread to the horrors to which Luc had been subjected after having been drugged and taken across the border from Venezuela and transported to the furthest flung regions of Colombia.

It was a story of courage during months of imprisonment, telling of his eventual escape, after a bitter fight, into one of the most sparsely populated regions of the world, where he had needed all his considerable physical and mental powers to survive in a hostile jungle environment.

Even then, if it hadn't been for the aid given by a small group of indigenous Indians who had nursed him through bouts of jungle fever and eventually taken him up river to a small settlement of gold prospectors, he might never have made it back to England.

Discarding the paper, Aphra stared into space, feeling sick as she recalled the way she'd greeted him on his return to Fairmead Hall. Bleakly she let her mind drift over the past days, realising how much her bitter words of recrimination must have wounded him. If only he'd told her the truth! But then, of course, her contentious attitude had hardly encouraged his confidence. Little wonder he'd taken an instant dislike to her.

Not that it mattered now. Kathryn, his real love, was back and had brought with her the greatest gift she could have given him—his own child. The fulfilment of all Amélie's hopes and desires.

The pain of loss a raw ache in her heart, Aphra stared sightlessly at the newsprint in front of her. Thank heavens she'd had the means to return to England, leaving Luc and Kathryn to enjoy their reunion without having to suffer the embarrassment of her unwelcome presence.

The soft buzz of the doorbell interrupted her thoughts. It was probably the porter returning with the goods she'd ordered to stock up the fridge, she surmised.

Padding on bare feet to the hall, she opened the front door, her polite smile fading as a furious Luc burst across the threshold.

'What the hell do you think you're playing at?' he thrust at her, his face taut and dark with anger. 'How dare you walk out on me like this?'

He pushed past her as if he owned the place, stalking past the half-opened bedroom door and making for the sitting room clearly visible through the glass-panelled door.

'I left a phone number where I could be contacted...' she began, her heart thudding with the shock of seeing him and the flood of tangled emotions his nearness engendered.

'A fat lot of good that was!' he growled over his shoulder. 'Your solicitor had never heard of Aphra Benchard, or Aphra Grantly, or Annie Glover for that matter. Under a certain amount of pressure he did admit to having a client whose first name was Aphra, but he had no intention of releasing her full name or her London address until he heard from her personally.'

'Then how...?' Aphra began desperately, having no recourse but to follow his long strides into the elegantly appointed sitting room and watch helplessly as he took up his position in the centre of the Aubusson carpet.

'By checking up on your first marriage certificate, Miss Beaumont-Valance,' he snarled. 'When you married Peter Grantly you gave this address as your place of residence.' Dark eyes raked across the elegant surroundings. 'My God, Aphra, is this how you get your kicks? Pretending to be some poor, misunderstood waif who has to earn her own living waiting on the old and infirm?' His brooding gaze, devoid of all understanding, accused her mercilessly.

'How dare you speak to me like that?' Briefly she registered the fact that Luc's journey back to England must have been accomplished a great deal quicker than her own. Closing the distance between them, she confronted him, fists clenched at her sides. 'What my parents own, they've worked for. That they share their wealth with me is my good fortune. But it doesn't stop me from wanting to find my own worth—'

'To give something back to society?' His mouth curled derisively.

'Don't you dare sneer at me, Luc Benchard!' Infuriated, Aphra lifted her closed fists and hammered on his chest, hating and loving him in a turmoil of unresolved emotion, her knuckles indenting the casual dark shirt which stretched across it. 'I love my work as a therapist. I enjoy being able to help people regain lost skills and I'm not going to apologise for that. After Peter died...' She stopped, seeing the look on Luc's face and finding herself at a loss for words.

'More lies, little Annie Glover, eh?' He grabbed at her stilled fists, enclosing them with iron hands. 'But nothing I didn't know from the moment I married you. I'm surprised you didn't realise that your status as a widow would be declared on the marriage certificate.'

'Oh!' She stared at him blankly. It was true. Everything had been done in such a rush she just hadn't registered the fact that her previous marital status would have been recorded. So all the time in Corsica when he'd taunted and teased her about her previous relationship he'd known its dissolution had been caused by death and not divorce.

Swiftly she rose to her own defence, hurt and bewildered that he'd taken fun in baiting her. 'So what? It didn't invalidate anything. You wanted to think of me as an immature divorcee. I just didn't bother to correct you. Besides,' she continued as she began to come to terms with the initial shock of his unexpected appearance, 'you weren't honest with me either. Why did you let me go on believing that you'd deliberately ignored your grandmother when all the time you'd been held incommunicado in some Colombian hell-hole?' She nodded her head in the direction of the newspaper strewn across the floor where she'd let it fall.

'Pride? Pique?' He drew her intractable form closer to his masterful body. 'All the wrong reasons, no doubt, but very persuasive ones at the time. I would have told you eventually.'

Aphra forced herself to give a dismissive laugh. 'Well, you've been saved the trouble. Like they say—I've read all about it.'

'Well, at least that's two misunderstandings cleared up.' There was an edge to his voice which disturbed her. 'Now let's try a third. Why did you run out on me?'

Her body stiffened protectively. 'You read my note or you wouldn't be here. What did you expect me to do? Be the spectre at the feast? Give me some credit for discretion.' To her horror she felt the hot weight of tears behind her eyes and rapidly blinked to clear them. 'The least I could do was to let you and Kathryn enjoy your reconciliation in peace.'

'What reconciliation, Aphra?' he demanded grimly. 'I don't know how long you stayed outside the cottage eavesdropping—'

'Long enough to know she still loves you and—' She'd been going to tell him that she also knew that Kathryn had borne his son, but as the words choked in her throat he interrupted her roughly.

'Kathryn has never loved anyone but herself! I finally realised that shortly after we started our South American tour. Perhaps it was spending so much time alone in each other's company, but it didn't take long before it dawned on me what a fool I'd been. We had nothing in common.'

'Except a mutual physical attraction?' Aphra suggested ironically, stunned by his unexpected renunciation.

'Not even that any more,' he denied flatly. 'Beauty without compassion soon loses its attraction and Kathryn only ever loved the reflection she saw in her mirror. Think about it, Aphra. If she'd had any humanity in her beautiful body how could she possibly have betrayed me like she did?' His voice was harsh, a dreadful bitterness mirrored in his obsidian eyes.

Where her heart should have been, Aphra felt only a curious cold numbness.

'When she married Felipe Carreira,' she whispered, stating it as a fact rather than a question.

'When she returned to the States in a tantrum because I failed to keep an appointment with her!' Luc contradicted tautly, releasing her chin with a gesture of disgust. 'You read the story. Didn't you wonder why no one reported me missing?'

'I thought you were alone—that Kathryn had already left you.' She gazed at his set face with dawning horror as she recalled the conversation she had overheard at the cottage.

'No.' He shook his head, his eyes fastened on her appalled regard. 'The original plan was for Kathryn to accompany me to a lecture I'd agreed to give at a town not far from the border with Colombia. But the previous evening she'd been invited to attend a celebrity lunch at a hotel in another town some sixty or so miles away. She wanted me to cancel my appearance at the seminar and escort her to the lunch instead.'

'But you'd already made your own arrangements. How could you cancel them at the last moment?'

'Precisely.' He nodded his dark head. 'Unfortunately Kathryn didn't share that point of view. She decided to go alone to the lunch and we arranged I'd pick her up there later the same night.'

'So when you didn't arrive on time...' Aphra paused as she felt a cool wave of horror begin to encompass her. 'She just packed up and left for the States, without trying to find out why you'd been delayed?'

'Yes.' His dark head dipped in terse agreement. 'In her eyes I'd already thwarted her plans for the day and she wasn't going to stand for any more disrespect. So she decided to punish me for being late by walking out on me, under the impression that I'd lose no time in following her laden with abject apologies and suitable gifts.'

'Oh, Luc...' Words failed her at the degree of Kathryn's petulance. 'And no one else realised you were missing?'

'No one,' he confirmed grimly. 'We'd already checked out of our previous hotel and both taken our own luggage with us, Kathryn choosing to travel to her lunch by a hired car, and we hadn't booked a hotel in Caracas. From then onwards our itinerary was unplanned, so no one was expecting us.'

'And when you didn't go back to Kathryn in the States as she'd expected, instead of trying to find out what had happened, or attempting to contact you in England, she married Felipe,' Aphra said quietly as the enormity of the consequences of such action dawned on her.

Luc nodded. 'To teach me a lesson—and believe me she did! She confirmed what I'd already discovered—that she was totally self-absorbed.'

Aphra sought for words to mitigate Kathryn's gross self-indulgence, but could find none as she realised how the other woman's silence had prolonged Luc's ordeal—might even have resulted in his death. 'But surely you had some identification on you?'

Luc shrugged. 'Everything was in the car. Passport, credit cards, luggage. Their only interest was me, or rather the American senator who happened to be driving the same model car and for whom they'd mistaken me. Their plan was to bargain for the release of one of their terrorists held in the USA. Once they'd got me out of the car they set fire to it and pushed it over the side of the mountain, so no clues were left which might betray them.'

Helplessly Aphra shook her head. 'If I'd had any idea what you'd been through when you arrived at Fairmead that evening, I would never have been so hostile,' she admitted bleakly.

'And if I'd known you were a grieving widow I would never have taken advantage of your pity and suggested this unholy alliance in the first place!'

She flinched from the venom in his tone. 'Why? It was a stupid deception, I admit, but it made no difference to the outcome. Our marriage was legal, and that was all that mattered at the time.'

'To you, perhaps. For me it was different. I loved my grandmother and I love Fairmead Hall, but I would have disappointed the first and lost the second if the only way to avoid doing so was to marry a complete stranger.'

'I don't understand...' Her bewildered gaze scanned the hard lines of his set face.

'You really don't, do you?' Luc sounded bemused as well as angry. 'Even though I didn't recognise you at first when we met again, I soon sensed that we were old antagonists.'

He gave a short, humourless laugh. 'When I finally realised who you were it was as if a curtain had lifted on the darkness which had overtaken my life. You were a part of my happy past, Aphra, the golden days when everything was going the way I'd planned it, and suddenly, instinctively I knew that I wanted you as part of my future too.'

Unable to make sense of his words, Aphra stared at him in amazement, her mind filled with a kaleidoscope of memories.

'What are you saying?' she whispered.

Luc gave a brief, ironic laugh. 'Quite simply that if I hadn't loved you I would never have asked you to marry me.' His eyes were narrowed slits in the hard planes of his face. 'And afterwards when I found out that you were a widow and not a divorcee, as I'd stupidly surmised and you'd let me believe, I was furiously, irrationally angry.'

He moved away from her, taking long, economical strides to the other side of the room before turning to face her as she gave a low moan of shock and disbelief.

'Oh, it's true, Aphra.' His voice was filled with a dreadful anguish. 'When I thought your previous marriage had been a mistake I was arrogant enough to believe that in time I could persuade you to love me. It wasn't as if we were total strangers, after all.' He paused to draw in a deep breath, while Aphra remained silent, her eyes fixed on the strained lines of his mobile face.

'That's the main reason I took you to Corsica. I wanted to get you away from Leamarsh and all your friends there, to have you to myself so that we could make a fresh start together. I was arrogant enough to believe that, given time and solitude, I could reawaken the past and persuade you to love me just a little in return.'

Luc had truly loved her? The pain that thrust through Aphra's heart was like a red-hot knife. Too much, too late... No, it was impossible to believe, and yet...

'That's why you baited me about sharing a bed...' she murmured wonderingly, understanding for the first time the reasons behind his taunts on their first night at the cottage.

'I wanted you to confess the truth about your past,' he agreed brutally. 'I felt cheated and angry. How could I compete with the memory of a man you had loved and who'd been torn away from you by death? At that moment I saw my dreams of our future together for what they were—illusions.'

'No!' Furiously Aphra gathered her strength to refute his hurtful lies as her memory reawakened with a vengeance. How had she believed for one trembling moment that he might have loved her when she had all the evidence she needed to prove otherwise?

'Don't insult me by pretending!' Her voice shook with distress. 'You were angry because you thought I'd deliberately deceived you for some wicked purpose of my own. Jealousy? Oh, no, Luc. Kathryn might have betrayed you but you were still desperately, passionately in love with her. All I could ever be was a substitute.'

The painful recollection surged to the front of her mind and demanded to be heard. 'What's the point of lying about it? After our wedding, when I was packing my case, you spoke about Kathryn, remember? You asked me how it was possible to go on living when you've lost someone you loved. You wanted to know what it was like when you couldn't reach out a hand and touch them. You asked me if the answer was to find a substitute and close your eyes when you kissed them!' An aching anger convulsed her as she recalled his bitterness, and the despair which had seared her heart at the emotive words.

'You don't have to lie to me, Luc. I went into this arrangement with my eyes wide open, and I'll walk away from it the same way. I promise you it won't cost you a penny.'

'You walked into it as blindly as Eros himself!' Luc accused her bitterly. 'Don't you understand anything? When I asked you those questions I'd just found out how you'd deceived me. All my plans to take you to Corsica, win your confidence and affection and seduce you slowly and gently had been shattered with that one word "widow".

'It was *you* I was speaking of when I asked you those questions,' he snarled. '*Your* reply I was soliciting. Think about it, Aphra. It was the discovery of your short and tragic relationship with Peter that had shattered my dreams and made me realise what a fool I'd been, not any lingering passion for an old and long-since-quenched flame.'

Stunned by the vehemence of his reply, she stared wordlessly at him, her heart pounding with disquieting intensity. Could he be speaking the truth?

What reason had he to lie? It would explain so much—his scathing passion, the harshness of his emotional response so at odds with the gentleness of his body. Their last night together he'd been everything she could have wished for in a lover and she'd imagined herself a substitute for Kathryn. Was it possible that Luc had cared for her after all?

She began to see the events of the past days with a whole new perspective, began to understand the reason for Luc's abrasive manner, the challenging anger which had threaded itself through their conversation, the heady mixture of desire and anger which had characterised their shared embraces.

Her mind in a spin, carefully she moistened her lips, seeking to choose her words with care. Somehow she had to make Luc understand that the love she had felt for Peter had been genuine but different—oh, so very different—from the powerful emotion which had filled—still did fill—every cell of her body when she was with him, Luc.

'Peter. . .' she began tremulously. 'Peter and I—'

'You don't have to explain.' Brutally he truncated her sentence. 'I should never have taken you to Corsica in the first place once I discovered the truth.' He gave a bleak, bitter laugh. 'And most certainly not have forced myself on you the way I did.'

'You know that's not true.' Scarlet flooded her cheeks. 'I wanted you as much as you wanted me. As for all the stupid misunderstandings, none of these need have happened if I hadn't gone out of my way to make your return a nightmare.'

She felt tears rise to her eyes and made a super-human effort to prevent their falling. 'I deserved your contempt, Luc. It was just . . . just that Amélie had seemed to be making such a good recovery, and I couldn't help wondering if I should have noticed something earlier, called a doctor in to see her. I suppose I wanted someone else to share the blame I thought was mine—and suddenly—there you were, the perfect scapegoat.' Her voice broke and she paused to regain her composure.

Slowly Luc shook his head. 'I should have realised you were reacting from grief. God knows, I owed you enough for all the loving care you'd lavished on my grandmother. Instead I insulted you and trapped you into marriage.' Bleakly he accused himself as Aphra gazed into his pain-filled eyes.

She essayed a weak smile. 'If you'd asked me outright about my first marriage I would have told you the truth—that I loved Peter as a dear friend but I would never have married him if he hadn't asked me to when we both knew he was dying of leukaemia.' She heard Luc's sharply indrawn breath as he moved towards her, felt his hands raise to embrace her, and gave herself the luxury of burying her head against his chest. 'We were married in his hospital ward, and he died shortly afterwards.'

'You mean that when we made love . . .?' His sombre eyes mirrored the horror of disbelief. 'That you . . . that I . . .' He choked into silence.

Aphra sighed. 'That you were my first lover—yes.'

'Oh, dear God, what have I done to you?' he demanded thickly.

'Given me a short but unforgettable holiday?' she suggested wryly.

'And every reason to hate me.' His face was a tight mask of despair.

'No.' She contradicted him quietly. Confession was said to be good for the soul, and although every word she was about to utter would sear her tongue with unbearable pain they had to be said. She owed Luc the truth even though there could never be a future for the two of them together.

'I love you, Luc,' she told him quietly. 'With every breath of my body and beat of my heart. Oh, it took me some time to realise it, and though I never hoped to replace Kathryn in your heart there was this tiny hope at the back of my mind that perhaps, when we returned to Fairmead and pretended to be a happy couple, in time the charade would become reality.'

'Aphra—' His face was transformed with a great happiness as he reached for her.

'No!' she cried passionately, stepping away from his embrace, her voice harsh with pain. 'It's too late for us. You can't desert Kathryn now. Whatever harm she did you in the past she still loves you, and she's the mother of your child—your son, Luc!' She saw him draw in an impatient breath and rushed on, denying him the privilege of speech, knowing he could never give up his own child. 'He'll need both of you, living together as a family...' She faltered to a stop, her voice wavering with painful emotion.

'You don't know what you're talking about.' Luc grabbed her upper arms and held them firmly.

'I do, I do,' she persisted stubbornly. 'I heard everything. How she married Felipe Carreira on the rebound and found that she was carrying your baby—'

'That was when you took to your heels, hmm?' His expression was unreadable.

Miserably she nodded. 'I couldn't burst in on you, and I'd eavesdropped too long. I just knew I had to get away, give the two of you the chance for a reconciliation.' She shuddered, remembering the anguish which had riven every cell of her body.

'You little fool!' There was affection mixed with irritation in his tone. 'If you'd only stayed a few more minutes you would have heard me explode that myth with the contempt it deserved.' He sighed heavily. 'There is no baby. There never was. Kathryn and I had ceased to be lovers months before she went back to the States. Even an egocentric like Felipe would have noticed a six-months pregnant bride; besides, children were never a part of Kathryn's plans, I can promise you!'

'But mistakes can happen . . .' Aphra's heart was pounding erratically.

'But not on this occasion,' Luc reassured her grimly. 'Kathryn soon admitted she was lying when she realised there was no way she could sustain the pretence. In reality she bitterly regrets her marriage to Felipe. According to her, she has fourth place in his life behind his car, his racing team and his fans, and she's not ready to settle for a life of domesticity.'

'But what did she hope to gain by lying to you?'

'Exactly what you were about to concede to her! A tender and passionate reconciliation, after which she would have admitted that our baby existed only in her imagination. It was a spur-of-the-moment ploy born of desperation when she realised I wasn't going to welcome her back with open arms.'

'But you can't be entirely sure...' Aphra protested weakly.

'I was sure all right,' he returned grimly. 'And it didn't take long to get the truth out of her when she realised I wasn't falling for a bizarre story like that. I promise you Kathryn has never given birth to any man's child, and if you still doubt it a phone call to Felipe in the South of France will confirm that fact.'

He sighed impatiently. 'Dear God, Aphra, how do you think I felt when I escorted Kathryn to the door of the cottage and found our breakfast abandoned on the shelf? I didn't know how much you'd overheard or seen—and then, when I got your note and realised that you'd run away...?' He glared down into her upturned face.

'And can you imagine how I felt when I saw *you* half-naked in the clutches of La Bella Bellini?' She could use Amélie's scathing name for the beautiful Kathryn with light-hearted amusement now she knew and accepted the truth.

'I'd only just struggled out of bed and made myself decent enough to answer the door.' Luc's stern mouth curved into a smile. 'I thought you were in the bathroom and the original plan had been to lie in bed and wait for you to come back to me.'

Aphra's heart quickened as an anticipatory shiver of desire lanced through her. 'Why would you do that?' she asked, opening her blue eyes wide in assumed innocence. 'Were you expecting to have your breakfast in bed?'

'Not expecting, hoping.' His gaze slid over the soft curves of her body as his voice thickened with desire. 'I love you, Aphra—every warm, soft, compassionate inch of you. I want to have you and hold you...' His arms encompassed her, his hands moving to explore the undulating lines of her waist and hips. 'I want to be husband, lover and father of our children...' She gasped as his soft mouth traced a line of sensuous kisses from her brow to her chin.

'It depends...' Deliberately she teased him, prolonging the electric tension which thrummed between them. 'There are a few conditions...'

'Name them!'

Unable to conceal her body's reaction as heat rippled beneath her skin at his touch, Aphra shuddered. 'I'd like to go on helping people like Amélie; teaching them how to speak again,' she said breathlessly. 'It's what I trained for.'

'As long as you don't neglect me and the children.' He nuzzled her neck with delicate kisses. 'Is that all, little Annie Glover?'

'Yes—no!' Quickly she corrected herself, her words coming in uneven jerks as Luc moved his body sensuously against her own, stimulating her rapidly awakening libido.

The heat of Luc's soft flesh beneath her fingers was sending shivers of arousal through her entire nervous system, and his response was leaving her in no doubt as to the power of his own need. She'd left the second condition to last, knowing he'd grant her anything at that moment. 'Never, *ever* refer to

me as little Annie Glover again,' she demanded
sternly. 'In future I'm Aphra Benchard, mistress of
Fairmead Hall.'

'And beloved mistress of Luc Benchard—now
and for ever!'

'Yes,' she agreed joyfully. 'Oh, yes, Luc!'

He swung her up into his arms and carried her
across the few remaining metres to the bedroom,
divesting her of the few garments she wore with
purposeful fingers, before inviting her to disrobe
him for her own pleasure.

She did so slowly with tenderness and controlled
caresses which had him groaning with frustration
as her cool fingers trailed across his burning skin,
before she spread herself out on the bed and invited
him to pleasure them both.

Together they discovered once more a rhythm
which united their bodies in one pulsating entity,
pure and thrilling, leading inexorably to the sweet,
explosive climax of mutual ecstasy.

Afterwards—a long time afterwards—satiated
with pleasure, Aphra stirred voluptuously in Luc's
arms. Perhaps here, in the beautiful but sterile
apartment her parents called home, she and Luc
had already set in motion the cycle which would
create a child—a real flesh-and-blood child who
would fulfil his grandmother's sense of destiny and
keep the Benchard name alive at Fairmead for
future generations.

Time had come full circle and Aphra sensed, with
a feeling of exultation, that somewhere, somehow
Amélie knew and was rejoicing.

'Happy' Greetings!

Would you like to win a year's supply of Mills & Boon® books?
Well you can and they're free! Simply complete the
competition below and send it to us by 31st August 1997. The
first five correct entries picked after the closing date will each
win a year's subscription to the Mills & Boon series of their
choice. What could be easier?

ACSPPMTHYHARSI

_____ _____

TPHEEYPSARA

_____ _____

RAHIHPYBDYTAP

_____ _____

NHMYRTSPAAPNERUY

_____ _____

DYVLTEPYAANINSEPAH

_____ _____

YAYPNAHPEREW

_____ _____

DMHPYAHRYOSETPA

_____ _____

VRHYPNARSAEYNPIA

_____ _____

Please turn over for details of how to enter ☞

How to enter...

There are eight jumbled up greetings overleaf, most of which you will probably hear at some point throughout the year. Each of the greetings is a 'happy' one, i.e. the word 'happy' is somewhere within it. All you have to do is identify each greeting and write your answers in the spaces provided. Good luck!

When you have unravelled each greeting don't forget to fill in your name and address in the space provided and tick the Mills & Boon® series you would like to receive if you are a winner. Then simply pop this page into an envelope (you don't even need a stamp) and post it today. Hurry—competition ends 31st August 1997.

Mills & Boon 'Happy' Greetings Competition
FREEPOST, Croydon, Surrey, CR9 3WZ

Please tick the series you would like to receive if you are a winner

Presents™ ❑   Enchanted™ ❑   Medical Romance™ ❑
Historical Romance™ ❑   Temptation® ❑

Are you a Reader Service Subscriber?   Yes ❑   No ❑

Ms/Mrs/Miss/Mr _____
                                                    (BLOCK CAPS PLEASE)

Address _____

_____

_____ Postcode _____

(I am over 18 years of age)

One application per household. Competition open to residents of the UK and Ireland only.
You may be mailed with other offers from other reputable companies as a result of this application. If you would prefer not to receive such offers, please tick box. ❑

mps MAILING PREFERENCE SERVICE   DMA   C7B